MONTEZUMA

ALSO BY B.N. RUNDELL

Rindin' Lonesome

Star Dancer

The Christmas Bear

Buckskin Chronicles

McCain Chronicles

Plainsman Western Series

Rocky Mountain Saint Series

Stonecroft Saga

The Quest Chronicles

MONTEZUMA

A QUEST CHRONICLES NOVEL
BOOK 4

B.N. RUNDELL

WOLFPACK
PUBLISHING
— EST 2013 —

Montezuma
Paperback Edition
Copyright © 2024 by B.N. Rundell

Wolfpack Publishing
1707 E. Diana Street
Tampa, FL 33610

wolfpackpublishing.com

Editing by My Brother's Editor

Paperback ISBN 979-8-89567-003-3
eBook ISBN 979-8-89567-002-6
LCCN 2024947008

To my ever-faithful wife of fifty-eight years. She has always been my partner, my friend, and my lover. Now, in these last few years, she added a new role—first line editor. Whenever I write a chapter or two or three, I read it aloud to her, and she adds her comments, if any, that helps me catch errors, mistakes, and poor wording. But that's the way it has been all our married life, we support one another, no matter the endeavor or the time or location. She has always been at my side, and even though these later years have added new challenges, we're here, we're together, and still madly in love. Thank you sweetheart! I couldn't have done it without you!

MONTEZUMA

1

SNAKE RIVER PASS

THE THUNDERSTORM HIT LIKE A STAMPEDING HERD OF buffalo. Thunder rolled across the heavens with such force it was felt in the ground beneath them. The lightning stabbed the dark skies, crackling with the roll of the thunder, splitting itself across the blackness in jagged lances that drove into the trees, slicing the tall timber and splitting smoldering branches that fell in pieces, leaving behind smoking stumps.

Cordell Beckett and Tabitha Townsend had pulled the collars of their dusters up, their hat brims down, and clutched at the reins, leaning over the pommels of their saddles. The horses plodded through the downpour, heads down, manes drenched and attitudes sour. The pack mule sided the grulla stallion, his long-time trail companion, and the flashy sorrel with flaxen mane and tail and four stockings, splashed along behind, carrying the girl that was having less than pleasant thoughts about her decision to accompany this man on their vengeance quest.

Cord lifted his head with every lightning strike, hoping to see any possible cover or retreat with each flash of light. They were on a rough road that was climbing into the mountains, and even though it passed as a stagecoach road, right now, it was no more than a muddy trickle of rainwater, making chuckholes with every rut. The sudden flash and crackle of lightning and thunder caused the animals to jerk their heads high, and Cord turned to look at the face of a rain- slickened cliff with a shadow below. He nudged Kwitcher, his grulla stallion, from the road, the lead line of the pack mule drawn tight, and he knew the high-stepping sorrel mare called Cassi would be sure-footed and follow close behind, with her precious cargo of Tabby.

Another flash of lightning showed the dark shadow to be at least an overhang, maybe a wide mouth entrance to a cave, but it would be shelter for man and beast and with the continued lightning flashes showing the way, the two riders and the animals moved under the overhang and paused, looking around, before sliding gratefully to the dry ground.

"Looks like this has been used before, they had fire yonder, and there's some dry wood. I'll strip the animals, if you'll get a fire goin', and some hot coffee would sure warm these cold bones!" chided Cord, grinning at the girl who lifted a wet face from under the drooping brim of her felt hat and tried to show a grin.

"I can do that, but first, I want outta this thing," she declared as she struggled with the wet duster. She shed the duster, the hat, and placed both on a big rock, and went to the woodpile to get the kindling and more for their fire. Cord set about stripping the gear from the animals, checking everything for any water damage, stacking the panniers and parfleches as close to the fire as possible and separated them to get some heat and dry off. The saddles were stacked with the bedrolls and he gave each animal a good rubdown with some dry grass and picketed them at the edge of the overhang. He slipped the rifles from the scabbards, and the coach gun from the packs and lay them against the big rock that held their dusters and hats, and after digging out some dry cloth from the panniers, he began to dry off each of the weapons. Though they were carried in full scabbards, water still managed to soak through and get the actions wet. He carefully dried each one, his Spencer with the telescopic sight, the Winchester Yellow Boy .44 caliber, the coach gun shotgun, and Tabby's Yellow Boy, taking them apart as needed, and standing them within reach when done. When he finished with the rifles and shotgun, he pulled out his Colt .44 and Tabby's Colt .36 pocket pistol, pistols they carried in holsters on their left hips, butt forward, under the dusters, for ready access, and began cleaning them thoroughly.

He moved closer to the fire, found a rock for a seat and sat with elbows on his knees as he watched Tabby preparing a meal, strip steaks hanging over the fire, pan bread rising nearby, and the coffee pot beginning its dance to perk the coffee. She had a pot of yampa and onions and Indian potato simmering at the edge of the coals. Cord asked, "That coffee 'bout ready?"

"Just about, a few more minutes, I reckon," answered Tabby, smiling.

They sat across from one another, letting the fire do its work of cooking their supper and warming the overhang, while lightning still crackled across the dark skies and thunder boomed and echoed over the mountains. They were on a trail that came from Georgetown, leading south into the higher mountains, and split about a mile and a half from town, with their chosen trail, the one less traveled, that turned west through a cut of the mountains, and soon bent back to the south, following a no-name creek and a faded crudely-lettered sign with an arrow that pointed south saying, *Snake River Pass, Montezuma, Coleyville, and...*but the bottom part had broken off and probably used for firewood by some passersby. It was a poor excuse for a stage road, but the stage line traveled this road, as weather allowed, once a week, or so, depending on any number of excuses.

As often happens to travelers, they stared into the fire and grew pensive. Cordell Beckett had been on the trail of the outlaws for most of two years, a trail that started in Missouri when his family had been murdered by so-called Red Legs or Jayhawkers, but the attack happened *after* the war and the Jayhawkers were supposed to be men that fought for the freedom from slavery, but Cord's father was a country church preacher, and his family had always been on the side against slavery. After Cord spent a little more than a year preparing himself with tactics, weapons, and other guidance from an experienced former officer of the North, he set out on the trail of the band of outlaws and had tracked them from Missouri, across Kansas, and into the gold fields of Colorado. His hunt had been partially successful, but dangerous. He had killed several of the men, all in fair fights and such, but he had also taken a few bullets himself. When his hunt took him to Oro City, Colorado territory, and on the way, he had overtaken some of the men, up to their usual dastardly deeds of stealing gold pokes and claims from honest men, and he brought Colt justice to a few. After that, the trail took him to Central City and Blackhawk, his path crossed that of Tabitha Townsend, when those same outlaws killed her brothers and prompted her to join Cord in his quest for vengeance and/or justice. As part of his hunt, while he was at Oro City and made a trek to Denver, he had been appointed as a deputy federal marshal by Marshal Shaffenburg, but lately, he had been a little remiss in his reports to the marshal. Not one to flaunt his badge, few knew he was a deputy, and his badge was usually kept in a pocket and out of sight.

Although the gang of Jayhawkers numbered about fifteen in the beginning, Cord had kept a list and knew the original number had been pared to about three or four, a number that varied by the new recruits to their ranks, but the tracks they followed from Nevada City showed they had been joined by at least three more riders. Cord still struggled with his quest, whether he was after vengeance or as part of his job as deputy marshal, if he was after justice. After seeing what they did to Tabby's brothers and others, the fires of vengeance flared up again, but with Tabby along, he had to be more careful than when he was alone.

He looked across the fire at the woman, young though she was, she was a very pretty girl and full of spunk and sass. If Cord had not allowed her to join him, she would have taken up the chase by herself, and he could not have that on his conscience, for she was beginning to grow on him. He was not more than a couple years older than Tabby, and she was a friendly sort, unabashed by his thoughts or ways, but not overly flirtatious. He had to admit there was a considerable mutual attraction between them, but he shook his head, concerned about her safety and uncertain about their future.

She looked at him across the fire, "You think we'll find any of 'em at Montezuma?"

"Well, hard tellin'. We don't have a trail to follow,

not with this storm," he lifted his eyes to the dark sky that was still spitting big raindrops, "but last we heard, they were headed this way and from what I've been told about the area, it seems like what they might think would be easy pickin's. We'll just have to see, if they're not here already, they'll probably show up here'bouts."

"So...in the meantime..."

"We get acquainted, learn about the area, the people, listen..." grinned Cord, sipping his coffee.

Tabby nodded, scooted forward to lift the lid on the pot and stir the vegetables. She slid the pan bread from the fire, letting it cool on the rocks, and lifted the strip steaks to check on their doneness, smiled and stripped them off the willows and lay them on the tin plates. She handed one to Cord, but he pointed at the pot for some vegetables and some bread, then passed the overflowing plate across to him. He sat it down beside him, waited for her to fill hers, and when she balanced the hot plate on her legs, he bowed his head and prayed a short prayer of thanksgiving and smiled as he looked up, "Dig in!"

She shook her head, "If you'da made that prayer any longer, I'da throwed a stick at you. I like my food hot!" she declared as she stabbed a piece of steak with her fork.

———

THE STORM SLID out of the mountains and down into the lower valleys about an hour before first light. Cord rolled over in his blankets, smelled the wet dog at his side and made a face, "Wheew, you stink, Blue!" he mumbled quietly, so as not to wake Tabby. The dog inched closer and Cord rubbed him behind his ears, rolled over and away from him and tried to get a little more sleep.

But sleep was elusive and as the sky faded from black to grey and the lanterns of the night snuffed out their lights, Cord slipped from his blankets, stretched, and with rifle and Bible in hand, went to the far edge of the overhang and found a big flat rock, where he sat for his morning time with the Lord. He was facing east, the narrow green valley with its no-name creek was below him, the higher granite-tipped peaks that stood well above timberline were across the valley and lined out at the head of this narrow draw, marching north and south as the backbone of the Rocky Mountains.

As the first light of day began to afford Cord a view of his surroundings, he smiled as he looked about, pleased with the majestic panorama. The stage road cut the trees below him and kept to the shoulders of the hills above the bottom of the valley, probably due to the snow accumulation in the bottom during the winter months. Above and behind him, a rugged talus slope fell from the jagged granite peak high above the valley. The head of the valley formed an expansive bowl surrounded by a collection of peaks, ridges, and talus slopes that reminded Cord of the palm of a giant hand, with the palm showing green across its breadth. It was a pristine setting, unmarred by the usual assortment of prospect holes from dream-filled miners.

He could see the trail they would follow as it bent across the shoulder and cut back across the face of the ridge behind them. He shook his head, thinking about a stage making that road, but that was not his problem to be concerned with now. He smelled coffee, smiled, and walked back into the overhang to see the smiling face of Tabby, sitting at the fire, frying up some bacon to go with the last of the pan bread from last night. They made short work of breakfast, saddled up and started on the trail in the clear mountain air made fresh by the storm, and the water had drained from the rocky trail and the footing was good for the animals. When they topped out on Snake River Pass, they stopped, stepped down and took in the magnificent view. Below them was another horseshoe basin that held the headwaters of Peru Creek in its palm. The creek and the valley bent back to the west and out of sight. Across the basin, a pin-point granite peak stuck its head high above timberline, cradling deep glaciers in its wrinkled face. Its arms stretched wide to show a smaller peak and ridge to the south, a higher ridge with snow-filled arms encircled the basin to join with the ridge where they stood. Far in the distance, past the nearby peaks, another long line of blue mountains marched north to south to frame the panorama that took their breath away.

They looked at one another, smiled and mounted up to continue their journey. The trail took them across the face of the wide talus slope that fell from the nearby peak and ended in the valley below, the valley that held the headwaters of Peru Creek. According to what Cord had learned, they would reach Montezuma sometime around midday, then their search would begin.

2

MONTEZUMA

ONCE THEY DROPPED OFF THE CREST OF THE PASS AND INTO the steep-walled valley, the trail sided the edge of the trees, staying above the Peru Creek, on the north side. The timber on the north side was sparse, compared to that across the stream. The dark skirts of black timber lay low on the shoulders of the high mountains that showed long talus slopes dropping from steep-sided peaks with massive rocky shoulders, topped off by the granite-tipped peaks that scratched the blue sky above. "Sure makes a man feel mighty small, lookin' up at them peaks and all," surmised Cord, glancing back to the petite woman on the long-legged sorrel with the flaxen mane and tail. As he looked at his companion, he was not certain which was the most eye-catching beauty, Tabitha and her dimpled smile, or the high-stepping, white-socked blaze-faced sorrel mare.

She flashed him a smile, turned her blue eyes to

take in the amazing scenery, knowing Cord was looking at her instead of the mountains, but that was alright, and it gave her a certain joy to know he liked looking at her. She chuckled to herself, *And he ain't bad to look at either!*

The green-bottomed valley stretched between the mountains, making its way west and eventually, after merging with other streams like the Snake River, would eventually make it to the flats and beyond. Sometimes, she wondered what it would be like just to follow the rivers all the way to the ocean, but for now, she enjoyed the cool mountain air and the breeze coming off the glacier-hoarding mountains.

The stage road crossed where the timber grew thick on both sides of the valley, took to the trees before rounding the shoulder to overlook the confluence of the Snake River and Peru Creek. From here the Snake would flow to the west and further down the long valley that would eventually come to the meeting of the Snake and the Blue River. The narrow Snake River valley isolated the settlements of Montezuma and Coleyville, with many prospect holes with dumps, and working mines littering the mountainsides.

"Are these gold mines?" asked Tabby, a confused look on her face. She and her brothers

had filed a claim and had a placer workings near Blackhawk, but those were different than what covered the faces of these mountains.

"No, I believe these are mostly silver mines. I was told that the early discovery was up that draw yonder," nodding to the southwest where a long valley split the mountains, "by a fella name of Coley, they named the town after him and then others learned this was silver country, although there had been some minor discoveries of gold, the most productive were the silver mines, with the biggest producer was that found by John Coley. But others came and found more, and a fella name of John Cullom discovered another'n and built a crude furnace to get the silver from the ore."

"Gold's easier. Just shovel the dirt in the rocker box or sluice, add water, and walla! Gold!" declared Tabby, remembering her time with her brothers.

Cord chuckled, "Yeah, and it's thinkin' like that what caused all these men to pick up and come to the mountains lookin' for that easy pickin' gold, but they found out it ain't that easy. So, many of 'em turn to outlaws, like those we're after."

"Think we'll find 'em?"

"Dunno, but gotta look an' listen, then mebbe so..."

They rode into the town, if it could be called that, side by side, looking about. Tabby had the collar of her duster turned up, her hair tucked in, and her hat pulled low. She looked at Cord, giggled, "We'ns prob'ly look like outlaws our own selves. You see the way some o' those folks are lookin' at us, all covered

up and such, like we're tryin' to hide ourselves in our
own clothes."

"Alright, alright. There's a hotel there, the
Summit House, and look there next to it, the Summit
Chop House. We'll get us some rooms, put the
animals in the livery across the street yonder, and
then we'll get us somethin' to eat and look around.
That sound good to you?"

"It do. I'm lookin' forward to eatin' somebody
else's cookin'," she giggled, glancing to Cord as he
nudged Kwitcher to the livery.

They stopped outside the big doors of the livery,
stepped down and Cord frowned as he looked into
the dark interior of the building, saw and heard a
man at the anvil and forge and stepped closer,
waited until the hammer stilled and called out, "Got
room for two more horses and a pack mule?"

The man looked up with a scowl, looked at Cord
from under bushy brows and motioned with his
hammer, "Stalls back there. Hay's in the corner, stack
the gear in the stall or put it in the tack room." He
turned back to his work and ignored Cord and Tabby
as they put their animals away. After stripping the
gear, they gave the animals a rubdown with handfuls
of hay, tossed it in the haymow and with weapons in
hand, bedrolls in the other, they walked across the
street to the hotel. It was a two-story clapboard
false-front building with peeling whitewash, and the
adjoining single-story shared the same clapboard
siding. The sign over the front of the hotel read

Summit House, and next door, a sign that sort of matched the other read, *Summit Chop House.*

Tabby had unbuttoned her duster, pushed the hat back on her head and smiled and laughed as they walked into the hotel. Cord went to the counter, "We need a couple rooms," he began, and saw the stern face on the woman behind the counter as she glanced from him to Tabby, who stood behind him, looking around.

"Two rooms?" she asked, looking at Cord with a glare that reminded him of a teacher from his youth.

"Yes, please," he replied, "and preferably close to one another."

That garnered a stern look and she turned to get a pair of keys from the pegboard behind her as she spoke over her shoulder, "Sign the guest book."

As Cord signed the book, she lay the keys on the counter, looked at his signature, looked up at him and closed the book without another word. She turned away as Cord picked up the keys, looked at the number and shrugged as he picked up his gear and pointed Tabby to the stairs. As they topped the stairs, Cord glanced back over his shoulder and down the stairs, turned to Tabby and said, "Sure is a friendly town, ain't it?"

"Hadn't noticed, guess I wasn't payin' attention," shrugged Tabby, taking the key to her room from Cord, looked at the number, saw the room and went to the door. "We gonna clean up, meet downstairs?"

"Sounds fine. You hungry?"

"I am, and I'm gonna have one of everything on the menu!" she declared and ducked into her room, giggling.

Cord smiled, shook his head, and went into his room. He dropped his gear on the bed, went to the washstand and poured water from the pitcher into the basin and after stripping off his shirt, he washed up, trimmed his whiskers, and with the aid of the mirror, combed his hair. He put on his clean shirt, dusted off his trousers and wiped the dust off his hat and picked up his light buckskin jacket that hung past his hips and easily covered his holstered pistol. Satisfied, he slipped on the jacket and went down the stairs to wait for Tabby. There was a pair of wingback chairs before the window, and he settled in one, to look around and wait. His first glance caught the clerk glaring at him as if he was some strange intruder, but she quickly turned away and Cord turned his attention to the window and the board-walk outside.

While he waited, he pulled out his list and looked it over. It was the same list he started with when he left Missouri and found one of the former leaders of the Jayhawks who told him about the others and gave him their names. He had several names crossed off, but there were others that remained of the first group and several new names added of recent recruits. He looked at the list, *Newt Morrison, Bill Coogan, Buck Smithers, José Espinoza,* and the most recent, *Yaqui, Chapo, and Gooseneck.* He wasn't too sure about the last two names, but thought they were the last two outlaws that joined. It had been a long ride and search and a costly one.

He had lost a close friend, Yellow Singing Bird, the Ute woman who had joined him in Kansas, and he had been wounded more than once himself. Now, he had company on his hunt, although he still had reservations about Tabby being with him, but he knew if he had not acquiesced, she would have taken up the hunt herself. She had lost her two brothers, the only family she had left after raiders had killed the rest of her family, and she had more grit and determination than most men twice her age and size. Cord chuckled at the thought, put the list away and heard steps on the stairs.

She had stacked her natural curly brown hair high atop her head, her scrubbed face showed dimples and a smile, her blue eyes sparkled with mischief and her fresh blouse with lace at the collar and neck was tucked into her mid-calf length split skirt and everything about her showed beauty, poise, and grace. Cord stood, smiling, wondering where this beautiful woman had been hiding ever since he first met her in Blackhawk. She came down the stairs and greeted Cord, "Well, sir, are we going to dine at the restaurant?" and giggled as she flashed a coy smile.

Cord nodded, extended his arm for her, and noticed she had a stole draped over her arms that covered her pistol that still rested on her hip. He

grinned, accepted her hand in the crook of his elbow
and started for the door. He opened it wide for
Tabby, followed her through and they stepped on the
boardwalk, paused to look around, and went to the
restaurant next to the hotel, stepped in and took a
table near the window. Cord, ever the gentleman,
pulled the chair out for Tabby, seated her and pushed
the chair in a little, took his own seat and doffed his
hat, laying it in the chair beside him. He looked
around the room, noticing the glares, stares, and
intentional turn aways from most everyone in the
restaurant. He frowned, but picked up the one-page
menu and began to look it over, wondering about the
cold reception from the town.

3

COMPANY

"Ever'body jes calls me Cooky! So, folks, new in town, are ye?"

"We are, and we're hungry, Cooky. So, what'chu recommend?" replied Cord, looking at the aproned pot-bellied man with thick sideburns, ruddy cheeks, and mostly white hair, what there was of it. Cord chuckled to himself, thinking this man reminded him of stories of Santa Claus.

"Oh, we got stew, an' we got steaks, taters an' such. Course tonight's steaks that're leftover become tomorry's stew, so there ain't much differ'nce," he cackled, wiping his hands on the already soiled apron, as he looked from Cord to Tabby. "How'bout'chu, little lady? Stew or steaks?"

Tabby smiled, "Oh, well, Cooky, I think I'll have the stew, assuming it has more than last night's left-over steaks."

Cooky grinned, nodding, "Oh it do, missy, but I ain't allus shore what all's in it, but it usually turns out good, an' so far ain't nobody died, or complained. Course them what died couldn't complain, so..." he shrugged as he cackled, making his belly bounce under the apron.

"Did you sample it while you cooked it?" she asked, smiling broadly and trying to keep from giggling.

"Oh sure, sure, gots to do that. Any cook knows that!" he declared, his brow furrowing with a dash of seriousness.

"An' you're still kickin' as well as cookin', so...I reckon I'll risk it!" answered Tabby, glancing from Cooky to Cord.

Cord added, "I'll try some, too, Cooky."

Cooky nodded, turned and stopped still when he saw two men coming in, and begin looking around the tables. They appeared to see the newcomers, then nudged one another and started toward the table. Cooky turned slightly toward Cord, and covered his face with a corner of his apron, "Watch out, trouble's comin'!" and nodded toward the two men before turning back and disappearing into the kitchen.

The two men were glaring at Cord and Tabby, and as they neared, both broke into lecherous grins, looking mostly at Tabby and coming closer. The bigger of the two stood just shy of six feet, probably weighed in at two hundred pounds, most of it hanging over his belt. Woolen britches hung from overstretched galluses that fought to keep the shirt-tails of the Linsey-Woolsey shirt contained. He had a holstered pistol hanging on his hip and a tarnished star on his pinstriped vest. As he neared, he cackled, showing a row of yellow teeth that looked like dull pickets on a backyard fence. His attention was focused on Tabby and he greeted her, "Wal, howdy missy. I see you made it, an' I been waitin' on you for a mighty long time!" he slobbered as he reached for her hand that she quickly jerked out of his reach.

The second man was smaller, uglier, and dirtier, and his teeth appeared to be missing every other one, but his lower lip was bloused by his slobbers and an apparent injury. His eyes flared and glared as he cackled, nodding his head and glaring at Tabby. When the first man stepped back when Tabby jerked her hand away, the smaller man cackled, slobbered, and mumbled, "Yeah, yeah, we been waitin', Willy said we'd share you! Hehehehehe," as he started to reach for her hand but Tabby pulled back closer to Cord.

"I think you fellas are mistaken," began Cord, putting his left hand on the table, his right hand across his chest and dropping to his pistol. He slid his chair forward, extending his hand to the men with his palm held out as if to stop or push the men back.

The bigger man, Willy, spoke to his partner,

"Now Harold, hold on..." and turned to look at Cord as he pulled the vest around to show his badge. "Now, see here mister, we's both the sheriff's deputies an' what we say, goes! An' it's our job to welcome newcomers, that's you, to town..." he paused, cackled as he nodded toward Tabby, "an' womenfolks get a special welcome. We'll just take her with us back to the sher'ff office an' give her a *gooood* welcome!" He turned away from Cord, started to lean across the table to grab Tabby.

Cord came to his feet, grabbed the big man by the long hair at the back of his head, and as Cord stepped from the table, he brought the man's head down to meet his upcoming knee, smashing his nose, breaking several of his front teeth, flattening and blousing his lips, and shattering many of the bones in his face with that one impact. Cord released his grip on the man's hair and let him fall to the floor.

The mousy partner was grabbing at his pistol but Tabby came to her feet, pistol in hand and brought it down on the partner's head, making him crash to the floor, unconscious. Cord looked at Tabby, both grinned and glanced around the room. Cord asked, "Is that the way you welcome all newcomers?" as he looked at the astounded people seated at the other tables.

One man shook his head, let a slow grin split his face, and started applauding. The others relaxed, and a few joined in the applause. Cooky came from the kitchen, although he had been watching over the swinging door, and added his clapping to the applause. One woman said, "We've been needing someone to do just that. But..." she shook her head, "the so-called sheriff has other deputies, so, this won't be the end of it."

Cord nodded, glanced at Tabby, "You wanna stay and eat or leave?"

"What, and miss out on Cooky's stew? I'm hungry," she declared as she sat back down. Cord looked at Cooky, "Got anybody that can lend me a hand taking out the trash?"

Cooky grinned, "Yeah, me!" and came to Cord's side. Cord grabbed the hands of the one called Willy while Cooky took Harold and they dragged the two unconscious deputies out the back door and dumped them behind the outhouses. Cooky looked at Cord, "There will be trouble, just so's ya' know."

"How many?"

"The sheriff's got two or three other deputies, and of course, he's trouble himself."

"The other deputies like this?"

Cooky chuckled, "Yeah, but they might not be too happy to find out what happened to those two."

"So, how'd you get a sheriff like that? You vote him in and..."

"Nope. We had a deputy name o' Pickens. Sandefur Pickens, Sandy, but most called him Slim, but slim he wasn't. One day he was here and our deputy, next day he was gone and Steele showed up. They din't waste no time goin' 'round to ever business, mine, and such, demandin' ten per-cent of their take. An' folks thought it easier to pay than fight, so..." he shrugged then added, "Even the cabin where Slim was livin' was taken by Steele and his men."

"Hmm, that's not good. Oh, well, we'll just hafta wait an' see what happens, then, won't we?"

"Oh, by the way, supper's on me!" declared Cooky as they stepped back into the restaurant. One of the other customers was putting away a pail and mop he used to mop up the blood, and with a grin, nodded to Cord and Cooky, then rejoined the others at his table.

It was early morning when they came downstairs and were greeted by the same stern-faced woman who greeted them the day before. She glared at the two, but spoke directly to Cord, "The sheriff said to tell you he wanted to see you 'fore you leave town!"

"Oh? Well, maybe after breakfast," responded Cord, glancing to Tabby and the door.

"He's not one to be kept waiting," growled the woman. "An' it's people like you that make it hard for the rest of us!"

When Cord glanced at the woman, he had to do a double-take, he thought he saw steam coming from her nostrils, but apparently not. He stepped to the counter, "People like us?" he asked.

"Yes! The sheriff works hard to make this a safe

town for all of us, and troublemakers come around and make things difficult for the rest of us!"

"So, now we're troublemakers?"

"Yes! I heard what you did to those two deputies! They were just trying to keep the peace and you had no call!" she whined.

"And what about the two deputies? Should I have let them take my lady and do whatever they had in mind? Is that what you call *keeping the peace?*"

The woman looked at Cord with wide eyes, turned to look at Tabby who was nodding her agreement, then back to Cord, "But, but, but..." she started, unable to make a reply.

"Ummhmm, and I suppose they've done that before?"

"Well..." she whined, trying to fidget with the ledger book before her, and avoiding Cord's gaze.

"My father used to tell me that the only thing it takes for evil to prevail, whether in a town or village or home, is for the good people to do nothing. Is that what you want? People like those two deputies having their way with the womenfolk and no one to stand against it?"

"Well..." she whined, "it's just..." she shrugged, still refusing to look at either Cord or Tabby.

Cord just shook his head, "Mmmhmmm," he moaned as he turned away. He smiled to Tabby, "How 'bout some breakfast?"

"Sounds good to me!" she answered and waited for him to open the door.

When they stepped into the *Summit Chop House* they were greeted by Cooky with a broad smile. "Well, good mornin' to my two favorite customers! What'chu gonna want for breakfast, you two?" he declared as he ushered them to the same table.

As they were seated, he lowered his voice, "The sheriff was in an' he ain't happy. He was askin' all about what happened, an' I tol' him you was just defendin' your lady friend."

Cord replied, "He left word at the hotel he wants to see us, or me, at least."

"Don't take no guff off him. I know those folks from last night'll be on yore side, so..." he shrugged. He glanced around, back to Cord and said, "Let me git you some breakfast," and trotted off to the kitchen.

He was grinning broadly when he returned with two plates, loaded with goodies. Cord and Tabby sat down their coffee cups as Cooky placed their plates before them. With eggs, bacon, biscuits, gravy, fried potatoes, their plates were overflowing and Cooky hurried off to get the coffee pot for refills. When he returned, he poured their cups full of the steaming hot brew and stepped back. He chuckled as he said, "Did muh heart good to see the sheriff all discom-bobulated like he was this mornin', but after what you done to Willy and Walter, he was not real sure about meetin' up with you. I cautioned him an' said, 'You better be careful, Sheriff. That fella, that's you I was talkin' 'bout, looked like he can handle himself purty good, after all, what he done to Willy, it happened so fast, most folks had no idea what happened! They just seen the two of 'em on the floor, stretched out 'n bleedin'." He chuckled, "Yessir, did muh ol' heart good!"

4

SHERIFF

"So there ya have it, Sheriff. Your deputies were rude and offensive and tried to take my woman and do who knows what? I was having none of it and thought to teach 'em some manners."

The sheriff leaned back in his chair, interlocked his fingers on his chest as he looked at Cord and asked, "So, if you're not prospectin', what brought you to Montezuma?"

"Well, Sheriff. I'm lookin' for some acquaintances." He reached into his vest pocket and withdrew his list and casually unfolded it, "Let's see here..." he began, and with a glance to the sheriff, began reading the names, "*Newt Morrison, Bill Coogan, Buck Smithers, José Espinoza, Yaqui, Chapo, and Gooseneck.*" As he read the list of names, Cord watched the sheriff for any response and saw a flinch when he read the first name. "Any of those names familiar to you?" he asked, folding the list and replacing it in his pocket as he looked at the sheriff.

"Why you lookin' for 'em?" he challenged, trying to appear casual.

"Oh, nuthin' important, just wonderin' where they might be nowadays. Been a while since I seen 'em, thought they might be around this part of the country."

The sheriff appeared to study Cord, then dropped his chair and leaned forward, elbows on his desk, and glared at Cord. "You look too young to have been in the war, you wasn't, was you?"

"No, Sheriff, I was not in the war, had to stay home and take care o' the farm for my mother and sisters. But..."

The sheriff held up his hand, "I figgered as much, but just what was your interest in these men?"

Cord grinned, dropped his eyes and looked back up at the badge toter, "Let's just say we had us a particular business arrangement."

"That's what I'm askin', what kinda business?"

Cord frowned, stared stoically at the sheriff, "Personal business, Sheriff."

The man leaned back, nodded his head, "I see. Well, couple things you need to know, first off, I ain't the county sheriff, that's Sheriff Gil Packer, he's o'er to Breckenridge. I'm kinda a deputy, or you could say, just a city sheriff, but..." he paused, took a deep breath, "My territory covers all up 'n down this valley. That includes Coleyville, Parkville, Kokomo, and more. So, if there's any *business* to be done, I need to be included. You see?" He leaned forward and drummed his stiff finger on the desktop where Cord had laid the list before putting it back in his pocket, "I know some o' those fellas. Rode with 'em back in the day! So, I've known 'em longer'n you and prob'ly know more about their *bizness* than you do!"

Cord frowned, "You rode with 'em?"

"Ummhmm," declared the sheriff, leaning back in his seat and interlocking his fingers across his midriff, grinning at Cord like the cat that caught the mouse.

"So...you knew Bill Tough?"

The sheriff nodded, grinning, "Ummhmm, an' others."

Cord retrieved the list, looked at the names that had been crossed off, "How 'bout Doc Jennison, Red Clark, Jim Lane?"

"Ummhmm, an' James Flood, Jack Hays, an'..." he leaned back, "lemme think, oh yeah, One Eyed Blunt, an' uh, Jerry Malcolm, an' Dave Poole. Then there was..." but before he could continue, Cord spotted the stub of a pencil on the corner of the man's desk and snatched it up and lifted the paper to write as the sheriff bragged about his former companions, "... Uh, Sam Wright, an' Moses Young, an' uh, Fred Wynkoop, an'..." he chuckled as he remembered, "... there was a dandy name o' Chauncey Tittle, but I heard he was dead, dunno though." He chuckled at the memory of his friends, glanced at Cord, and frowned when he saw him writing the names on his list.

Cord looked at him, "So, these others were with you when you made the raids in southeast Kansas and into Missouri?"

The sheriff, according to a name plate on the desk, Byron Steele, frowned, "Why?"

"Well, these others were there and if you weren't, then..."

"Yeah, I was there! What diff'rence it make? I was in on all of 'em till we split up after the Missouri raids. I come west, some o' the others said they was comin' too, but just me'n Willy Sherman came, he's the one you made a mess of last night."

"So, he's been with you a few years?"

"Ummhmm, but he just wouldn't keep his hands to himself. Mebbe now he might learn," grumbled Steele. The sheriff frowned as he leaned forward and pointed his finger in Cord's face, "But it's not your job to try to teach my deputies some manners, understand?"

Cord leaned back, smiled and held up both hands, palms forward and responded, "Sure sheriff, I understand. You'll do all the teachin' of manners from now on, that right?"

"Yeah," growled the man, nodding his head and waving at Cord as if to dismiss him from the office.

Cord nodded, rose, and said, "By the way, sheriff, let me know if you run into any o' these fellas, and I'd prefer you not tell 'em I'm around. You see, some of our business includes the settling of old debts and they haven't settled up just yet."

The sheriff let a grin split his face, "And you're here to collect?"

"You might say that," responded Cord, nodding and turning to leave. And as he turned, the sheriff called out, "And keep a short leash on that woman of yours. I understand she's the one that split Harold's head last night."

Cord nodded and pulled the door shut behind him, grinning to himself and thinking, *If you only knew, Sheriff, if you only knew.*

As the door closed, another door from the back room opened and another badge toter came into the area where the sheriff sat behind his desk, hands clasped behind his head as he leaned his chair back against the wall, staring at the door and thinking about the man that just left. When the new man entered, the sheriff looked at him, "Elmer, I want you to keep that man in sight! I wanna know where he is at all times, unnerstan'?"

"Yeah, sure, Sheriff, I can do that!" retorted the sniffler, who wiped at his nose and looked at the sheriff from the corner of his shifty eyes. "Why?"

"I don't trust him, he looks crooked to me."

Elmer cackled "Ain't we all? Hehehehe" he snickered as he shuffled out the door.

———

CORD STEPPED INTO THE RESTAURANT, spotted Tabby at the same table, and as she waved to him, he smiled and went to her side. As he seated himself, Cooky arrived, coffeepot and cups in hand and greeted Cord, "Mornin' friend, how'd your visit with the sheriff go?"

Cord chuckled, "So, he's not the county sheriff, just the Montezuma sheriff?"

"Self-appointed. But he sometimes claims more'n Montezuma," grumbled Cooky, sitting down at the table with the two newcomers.

"So, does Sheriff Packer know about this?"

"Dunno, ain't never seen him hereabouts. He purty much stays to the county seat, that's where his office is an' from what folks say, he don't like to leave his office much."

"Is he honest?"

"Dunno that either," Cooky shrugged, reaching for his own cup of coffee, glancing around at the empty restaurant. It was mid-morning, and the lunch crowd had yet to arrive. He looked at Cord, "Didja learn anything?"

"Ummhmm, the sheriff used to ride with the Red Legs."

Tabby scooted forward, looked at Cord with wide eyes, "He didn't, did he?"

"Ummhmm, knows ever' one of the names on my list an' then some. I think he's expecting them to show up just anytime now. He didn't say, but I think he's been in contact with them."

"What'd he say about you fixin' his deputies the way you did?" asked Cooky, not interested in the Red Leg talk.

"He asked me not to try teaching any of his deputies any more manners," he chuckled.

"Manners? That's what you call it?" asked a stunned Cooky as he leaned across the table to look at Cord.

"Ummhmm, I said I'd leave that up to him as long as they behaved."

Cooky shook his head, looked at Tabby, who was smiling at Cord and back to Cord, "If that don't beat all."

"So, Cooky, how far to Breckenridge?"

"A good day's ride, why?"

"I was thinkin' 'bout goin' down there, talkin' to the sheriff, use their telegraph, they have one, don't they?"

"Yeah, they have a telegraph, can't say much for the sheriff, though."

"Good," answered Cord. He looked to Tabby with uplifted eyebrows in a questioning expression, and she nodded, smiled, and pushed her chair back to stand. Cord stood, looked at Cooky, "We'll be back, Cooky."

"Good, things was gettin' kinda dull 'round here 'fore you showed up!" he cackled as he stood to return to the kitchen.

————

CORD DID his best thinking in the saddle. Although the surrounding country was amazing in its beauty and Tabby enjoyed the sightseeing, Cord rode in silence, wondering if he was getting himself too deep in the pursuit of the Jayhawkers. If there were more of them with Sheriff Steele, and if they met up with Newt Morrison before Cord found Morrison, he might be facing overwhelming odds, and with Tabby at his side, he would be endangering her as well.

The stage road to Breckenridge followed the Snake River west into the big valley that held the confluence with the Blue River. The stage road forked, with the north branch going to Georgetown, and the south branch going to Breckenridge. They rounded the flanks of Swan Mountain in the early afternoon and found shade in the trees for a brief rest and some coffee and jerky, letting the horses have a roll and some graze.

Tabby looked at Cord as he stoked the fire to get the coffee going and asked, "You've been quiet, is something wrong?"

He looked up, almost surprised at her question, then answered, "No, nothing wrong. Just contemplating what I learned and what we might be in for, since the sheriff said he rode with the Jayhawkers, we can't count on him backing us up against the others, and I don't want to put you in danger."

Tabby came to her feet, her fists on her hips and her head cocked to the side as she fumed, "Cordell Beckett - you're not *putting* me anywhere! It's my choice, and I'm going with you! And I told you before," as she shook her finger at him, "and don't you try to stop me!" she glared, daring him to challenge her declaration.

He let a grin fill his face, as he slowly shook it side to side, "I know, I know, and if I did try to stop you, you'd prob'ly do to me like you did that fella last night!"

"You darned tootin' I would!" she growled, giving him a daring stare as she sat back down, fuming and glaring at him.

He chuckled, laughed, "You sure are a purty thing when you get riled!"

She could not help but break into a smile and a bit of a giggle as she looked at him out of the corner of her eye and asked quietly, "You think so?" and giggled.

5

BRECKENRIDGE

MOST OF THE BUILDINGS ON THE MAIN STREET OF Breckenridge were of log, two showed a false front of clapboard, and many were vacant and windows and doors covered with rough boards. Most of the buildings were on the east side of the road and backed up to the Blue River. One two-story log building had a long sign that read *Fisk's Hotel* and had restaurants on both sides, while across the street was one of two liveries and blacksmiths. It was evident the original gold rush boom had faded and many buildings that had held businesses were now vacant. There were three saloons that were still open, and the miners had finished their day and were filing in for their nightly eats and drinks.

Cord nodded to the livery opposite the hotel and pointed out the sheriff's office on the left of the restaurant, "We'll put up the horses and mule, get us a room, maybe stop at the sheriff's office, or...just get us somethin' to eat." He shrugged as Tabby looked his way, smiling, and nodding her agreement.

The hillsides around the town had been stripped of trees for buildings, homes, sluices and more, leaving behind stumps, rocks and prospect holes with scattered dumps. Everywhere they looked, there were signs of previous prosperity but now they stood as grave markers of the past. As Cord and Tabby walked across the street to the hotel, he glanced to the sheriff's office, saw no light nor activity, and suggested, "How 'bout we just get us a room, have some supper, and look for the sheriff tomorrow?"

Tabby smiled, "Sounds good to me, I'm a little tired after that ride."

———

As THEY ATE, Cord looked around at the other tables, saw only two occupied and those by men who were obviously miners. There was nothing unusual about anyone nor any overheard conversation. It was a pleasant change from the open hostility of Montezuma, but this was obviously a town on the decline. When the cook returned to their table with the coffee pot in hand, Cord asked, "There's a telegraph in town, isn't there?"

"Yes, yes, it's next to the sheriff's office, but there's no one there now. The telegrapher is a woman and she, well, she keeps her own hours," he shrugged. With the cups full, he returned to his kitchen and Cord reached for his cup just as Tabby nodded to the window and said, "That big man on the bay looks familiar."

Cord glanced at the window, did a double-take and frowned, "That's Newt Morrison. He's the leader of the bunch that hit your claim."

Tabby's anger flared and she started to rise, but Cord stopped her with a hand over hers and said, "Don't - not now. We'll have to pick our own time and way. He's got several men with him and it's too risky. We'll talk to the sheriff tomorrow, then we'll decide what to do. I'm bettin' they're headin' to Montezuma anyway."

"I've been wantin' to get him in my sights ever since..." growled Tabby, slowly shaking her head and looking to the window.

"I know, I know, but we don't wanna lose him either. Let's finish our supper with some o' that pie the cook was talkin' about and then get us a good night's sleep. Tomorrow's soon enough to get everything started."

―――――

THE CROWD in the Lucky Boy saloon was no more raucous than usual, the miners, prospectors, and the usual hangers-on were bellied up to the bar and others gathered around the few gaming tables, but in the darker corner by the window that showed nothing but darkness, were five men, all strangers to the locals. They hunkered over their drinks, grumbling to one another, for they had been on the trail for the last two days with little rest and nothing but promises to drink. "I thought this was s'posed to be hoppin'! Ain't nuthin' but a bunch o' tired ol' sourdoughs tryin' to drown their sorrows!" growled the skinny man with a beak for a nose and eyes set closer together than a lizard with skin that reminded those around the table of that same lizard.

"Ah, Gooseneck, we just got here, ain't seen nuthin' yet!" whined the other narrow-faced man across the table. Whiskers covered his chin and long sideburns hid his ears, giving him the look of a skinny marmot with skin about the same color. Buck Smithers had been with Newt Morrison for almost as long as Bill Coogan and after James Flood was put under, back at Nevada City. Buck glanced at Newt Morrison who was hunkered over his mug of beer, staring into the brew, and Buck was always afraid of Morrison when he got 'notional' with too many beers under his belt.

Newt looked up at the others, "Yaqui, you sent Jose and Chapo to take the horses to the livery, that right?"

"That's what you said to do, Newt, so they done it. Should be back real soon."

Newt nodded, looked around the table at the four men, leaned forward and said, "Look, we're gonna stay here tonight, ain't no rooms in the hotels, but we'll stay in the loft of the livery, better'n sleepin' out in the rain. Tomorrow we'll look things over, an' if they ain't any better'n what we already seen, we'll move on to Montezuma and that country. We was tol' this was gold country, but looks like most o' the gold's done been got, folk's are leavin' and the town's dryin' up too, but we'll see tomorrow."

"Din't you say we might be meetin' some more men here?" asked Bill Coogan, frowning at their leader.

"Yeah, but from what the fella at the livery said, Steele has moved on, prob'ly up to Montezuma. There was a couple others I thought we might find, Moses Young, Sam Wright, an' Chauncey Tittle. Ain't surprised Chauncey ain't here, he's more into the city folks, this ain't fancy 'nuff for him." Newt looked around the table, "Any of you remember Sam and Moses?"

No one moved other than to look at each other, Newt grumbled, "Alright. You stay here, wait for Jośe and Chapo, then go to the livery. Yaqui, you come with me, we'll check a couple other saloons, see if we find Sam and Moses. We'll meet you back at the livery," stated Newt, coming to his feet. He turned his back on the others and strode from the saloon, Yaqui close behind.

They went to the Big Nugget, stood at the bar nursing their mugs of beer as they looked the crowd over, but it was not a big crowd and they soon were leaving, bound for the Mother Lode. As soon as he stepped in, Newt heard the deep bass voice that was familiar and he looked at a table with several men, all holding cards and playing poker. A big man, broad-shouldered and making the chair he was in look frail and little, chuckled and said, "I'll see your ten and raise you another ten!" The big man was black as midnight and broad as the caboose on a train, but he was all muscle and his deep voice reverberated around the crowded room. The game had drawn some spectators who wanted to see the winner of the big pile of coin, bills, and some nuggets, in the middle of the table.

The dealer leaned forward, "Alright gents—cards?" and worked his way around the table as several asked for cards, but two men folded and leaned back to see the outcome. The three men left in the game included the big Black man, a mine owner in a business suit with the collar undone and sweat on his forehead, and a rough-looking prospector with a full face of whiskers, beady eyes, and broad shoulders that strained at his galluses and tight Linsey-Woolsey shirt. The first man said, "I'll check to you," nodding to the man on his left. The dude wiped the sweat from his brow, and tried to look confident but fear showed in his eyes, as he said, "I'll call," and looked at the big Black man. A deep rumble rolled from the Black man as he chuckled, and slowly spread his cards on the table, "Full house, aces o'er eights!"

One of the watchers mumbled, "Dead man's

hand!" and others nodded. When the other two threw in their cards, admitting defeat, the big Black man let a belly laugh rise from the cellar of his broad chest as he leaned forward, a smile splitting his face from ear to ear and showing white teeth against the midnight skin, and he raked in his winnings. The others shook their head, stood, and mumbling to themselves, strode from the saloon.

Newt and Yaqui moved to the table, Newt chuckling as he came alongside the big Black man, "Moses, Moses, Moses. I see you're still rakin' in the winnings!" he said as he seated himself opposite the big man.

With a deep belly laugh, Moses recognized Newt and answered, "Ain't no sense loosin' when you don't have to!" He looked at Newt again, "I heard some o' the gang might be 'roun' these parts."

"That why you're here?" asked Newt.

Moses grew serious, shook his head, "No sir. I'm just makin' the rounds of the gold camps an' findin' it easier to get gold thisaway and not get dirty diggin' in the dirt!"

"You must be doin' alright, if this," motioning to the table and the winnings he was stacking and counting, "is any indication of what'chu been doin'," surmised Newt.

"It is, and I am. Sometimes they don't wanna let a Black man get in the game but when I says, *But boss, ain' my money as good as other'ns?* and they think I'm as dumb as a rock, their eyes get big when they see my roll and they get just as greedy as the next man. Then I usually clean up!" he chuckled, with the deep belly laugh rolling across the table.

"Seen any others?" asked Newt, looking around the room.

"Ain't seen a one, 'ceptin' you now."

"We'll prob'ly be goin' to Montezuma, it's not a gold camp, but they've got some new discoveries of silver and sounds like they might be the next boom town. You might remember Byron Steele? I hear he might be there ahead of us, so, we'll be lookin' it over soon. You'd be welcome to join us, if'n you were of a mind," suggested Newt.

"I'll remember that, but if I show up, don't act like you know me, leastways not till I fleece the locals," he said with a grin.

Newt and Yaqui rose, left the saloon to return to the livery, and as they walked, they were quiet, both thinking about Moses and Montezuma and what might lay ahead for them.

6

PACKER

Marshal M.A. Shaffenburg,

As previously discussed, seven of the original Jayhawkers have met their end. Others have since been recruited and their outlaw ways continue, now under the leadership of Newt Morrison, along with two of the original group, Buck Smithers and Bill Coogan. Recent recruits include José Espinoza, and three others that I only have first names for—Yaqui, Chapo, and Gooseneck. I am in Breckenridge to meet with Sheriff Gilbert Packer concerning his deputy, Byron Steele, who oversees Montezuma and the surrounding area. However, I believe Steele to be a former member of the Jayhawkers and other names have been given—Sam Wright, Moses Young, Fred Wynkoop and Chauncey Tittle. These names were supplied by Deputy Steele, thinking I was with them.

After I speak with Sheriff Packer, I will return to Montezuma and continue my pursuit of the outlaws. If you would find it possible, please forward warrants for the above named men. I will send a telegram with similar info to expedite the search.

Cordell Beckett

CORD LOOKED THE LETTER OVER, FOLDED THE PAPER AND slipped it into the envelope. After sealing the envelope, he addressed it to Marshal Shaffenburg, and with Tabby at his side, gave the letter to the clerk at the stage station for mailing. "Will that go out today?" asked Cord.

"Uh, yeah, haven't heard anything 'bout the stage, so that's good. Yeah, it'll go out today and get to..." The clerk looked at the letter, glanced to Cord and back to the letter, "Denver tomorrow, providin'..."

"Providin'?" asked Cord, eyebrows raised.

"Providin' it don't get robbed or sumpin'. Had that happen a time or two, so, ain't got no control 'bout that," shrugged the clerk, dropping the letter into the mailbag that hung at the edge of the counter. He looked up at Cord, "anythin' else?"

"No, that's all." He looked across the room to the opposite counter that had a screen over the top and resembled a bank counter, but the sign read, *Western Union Telegraph.* Cord nodded to the empty chair and desk behind the counter,, "Will anybody man that sometime today?"

"Uh, yeah, she usually gets in 'round ten or so. Keeps her own hours, but that thing rattles whenever it wants, whether she's here or not."

Cord glanced back to the station clerk, nodded and he and Tabby turned from the counter to leave. The clerk called out, "But if'n you wanna leave a message, I'll give it to her when she comes in, you can leave the money or come back an' pay it. But it won't go out without bein' paid."

Cord nodded, glanced to Tabby and said, "Reckon I will," and stepped to the counter, took up the pencil and pad and began to scratch out a condensed version of the letter:

Marshal Shaffenburg,

Need warrants for Jayhawkers Newt Morrison, Buck Smithers, Bill Coogan, José Espinoza, Yaqui, Chapo, Gooseneck, Sam Wright, Moses Young, Fred Wynkoop and Chauncey Tittle.

Also believe Sheriff Byron Steele to be part. Send warrants to Breckenridge c/o Sheriff Gilbert Packer or send to me at Montezuma. Cordell Beckett.

When Cord finished writing, he slid to paper under the screen, looked at the rate card posted on the wall and put a twenty-dollar gold piece on top of the gram. He looked up at the clerk who was watching and said, "I put enough on there to pay for it. Tell her I want it to go out immediately and that I'll be back later to check on it."

"Yessir, I will do that."

"Good," responded a stoic Cord as he glanced to Tabby and nodded to the door. They left and turned down the boardwalk to go to the sheriff's office and jail.

The sheriff was sitting on an armchair that he had leaning against the building, his feet off the walk, and his thumbs tucked in the pockets of his vest, as he surveyed the town and people. He saw Cord and Tabby approaching and looked at them through squinted eyes and wire-rimmed glasses that hung on the end of his nose. "Mornin' folks. You're new, ain'tcha?"

"We're new to Breckenridge, but just visiting. Want to talk with you, sheriff, and it might be better to be inside, if that would suit?" replied Cord.

The sheriff pushed against the wall, dropped the chair to all four legs, stood up and motioned to the door, "After you," and followed Cord and Tabby into the dimly lit interior. It was a typical office with three windows, one beside the door and one on each side wall. A solid door with a metal bar and latch was in the middle of the back wall, apparently leading to the jail cells. The sheriff motioned them to the chairs before his desk and walked around behind the desk to take his seat. He leaned forward with elbows on the edge of the desk and asked, "Now, what can I help you with?"

"I'm Cordell Beckett, and this is my friend, Tabitha Townsend."

The sheriff extended his hand across his desk, "Pleased to meet'chu, I'm Sheriff Gil Packer."

"I was just a little curious, Sheriff. We were up to Montezuma, looking for some men I ran into before and stopped by your deputy's office there," Cord paused as the sheriff held up his hand.

"Uh, hold on. I don't have a deputy up there. Did have, but county wouldn't pay him, so...well, he said he'd stay on, but haven't heard from him in a while, so I just figgered he went prospectin' or..." he shrugged. He looked up at Cord and continued, "Not that I couldn't *use* a deputy, but haven't been up there to find one quite yet. Summit County is the biggest county in the territory, covering most all of the northwest quarter of the territory, and several towns, settlements, and more. I could prob'ly use a half-dozen deputies, but the county ain't seen fit to provide 'nuff money to pay 'em, so..." he shrugged, holding both hands out to the side, palms up as he grinned.

He continued, "So, this *deputy* you're talkin' about. Tell me more."

"We had a little run-in with some of his deputies, seems he has several, when they tried to take my lady from our table in the restaurant and take her back to the office for their *entertainment*. But..." he chuckled as he glanced to Tabby and grinned, "we did not see that as any way to treat a newcomer in town, so we did not allow that."

Tabby picked up the tale as she scooted closer to the desk, "When the big one tried to grab me, Cord *convinced* him to keep his hands to himself, and after his face met Cord's knee, he agreed. But the other deputy tried grabbing me, and I tried to knock a little sense in him and teach him some manners and tapped him lightly on his noggin with my Colt. I think he was *convinced* also, but they were still sleepin' when the men dragged them from the restaurant."

Cord chuckled, "And the next morning, the deputy left word at the hotel and the restaurant that he wanted us to stop by his office, which we did, and that's when we learned about his *practices*. It seems that the businesses, mines, gold-diggers, and others are required to pay him ten percent of their take, for his *expenses*."

The sheriff pursed his lips, leaned back and looked from Cord to Tabby. "Interesting, interesting. Does it work?"

"Well, apparently, most pay, reluctantly, because if they don't, the badge toters take it and more."

"So, the people are not happy about it?"

"You could say that, at least none of those we met, and I can't see how anyone would be happy about it."

"So, what are you asking me?"

Cord looked at Tabby who hung her head, slowly shaking it side to side. They had talked about this and she thought the sheriff would do nothing, but Cord wanted to think he would respond with some action, but did not venture a guess at what. Now he knew she was thinking she was right when she said nothing would be done. Cord looked back at the sheriff, "Well, sheriff, I guess what I'm asking is if you knew about it, and what you might do about it.

"No, I did not know about it, and like I explained to you before, I have a mighty big territory to cover and the county does not see fit to give me the money to do it, so, the way I look at it, is if the people don't want to do anything, why should I?"

Cord glanced to a grinning Tabby and turned back to the sheriff, "Then you might be getting some warrants from Marshal Sheffenburg in Denver City. They will be sent here to await pickup by me. I would appreciate it if you would hold them for me."

The sheriff leaned forward on his desk, scowling at Cord, "And why should he be sending warrants here for you?"

"I asked him to."

"Why?"

"The warrants are for former members of the Kansas Jayhawkers that continued their outlawry after the war was over and have done that throughout Colorado gold country. Some of them are in Breckenridge now, and others are expected in Montezuma. They have been robbing and killing from Kansas into Colorado and will continue until they are stopped—hence, the warrants."

Cord and Tabby stood, turning to leave, but the sheriff said, "Hold on! Why is he sending warrants to *you?*"

"I asked him to," responded Cord, and turned his back to the sheriff and escorted Tabby out of the office, leaving the sheriff standing, frowning and waving for them to come back, but they were headed to the livery for their horses, hopeful of making it back to Montezuma before dark.

7

RETURN

THEY FOLLOWED THE STAGE ROAD FROM BRECKENRIDGE AS it sided the Snake River and bent around the flanks of Independence Mountain, turning south toward Montezuma. The sun was beginning to hide itself behind the towering peaks, but it would be several hours before dusk bid its goodbye to the day.

"Are we going to stay in the hotel again?" asked Tabby as they rode side by side on the stage road. Tall timber climbed the mountain to their right, and the valley dipped to the river on their left. The steep hillsides east of the river showed black timber basking in the last of the sunshine as the tall pines and spruce climbed the steep slopes of the mountains.

"No, I don't trust the sheriff and his cronies. What we want is to catch 'em away from town, and they're likely to be *collecting* their *taxes* from the prospectors and miners south of town, or up the

valley to Coleyville. The hills east of town beside
Morgan Gulch are covered with claims, many of 'em
active, and we could find us a campsite up that
gulch, maybe with some water, or up toward
Coleyville, but what I understand about Coleyville is
the main claim or lode was recently sold to a Boston
Silver Mining Company and there's not too many
other claims. So, I'm thinkin' the outlaws would
prefer the smaller claims, fewer miners, easier
targets."

"I see what you're thinkin'. If we lay in wait for
the *collectors*, we won't have to face the whole gang
and can take 'em, two or three at a time!" She
chuckled as she looked at Cord. "Good thinkin'!" She
grinned. "So, where we gonna camp?"

"Well, we're about to cross the river, so after we
cross, let's head up into the trees, see if we can find a
shoulder or a patch of aspen where we can make
camp."

———

AND THEY HAD CHOSEN WELL. A bit of a basin in a
cluster of aspen with a little spring-fed creek and a
shoulder that rose above the town and the valley
below. Cord had walked to the crest of the shoulder,
and in the dim light of early morning, he chuckled as
he looked over the shadowy valley and back to their
camp. Their chosen site was totally obscured from
the town and far slopes by the aspen-covered

shoulder where Cord sat, leaning against the dusty white bark of a big quaky with its fluttering leaves overhead. But the shoulder also afforded them a view of the town, the upper valley, the road climbing the far hills toward Coleyville, and the switchback trail that climbed the west-facing slope beside their encampment.

He looked over the shadowy valley, wondering what the day would bring, and opened the Bible that lay in his lap and began to read, choosing his father's favorite book and verse, Joshua 24:15 *And if it seem evil unto you to serve the Lord, choose you this day whom ye will serve; whether the gods which your fathers served that were on the other side of the flood, or the god of the Amorites in whose land ye dwell: but as for me and my house, we will serve the Lord.* Cord remembered the many times he heard his father quote that verse, at least the last portion, especially when there were so many around them who had been struggling because of the war and were tempted to leave and go west away from the war and the people that were so caught up in the fighting. Yet his father would often say, *"Son, when the trials and tribulations are at their worst, that's when the people need God the most. And it's our job, mine as pastor, yours as my family, to show those around us the truth of the promises of God."*

But Cord took a deep breath, remembering the time when the Red Legs attacked their home, killing everyone and burning everything, stealing whatever they could find. Cord had lain in the underbrush in the woods, watching helplessly as the renegades destroyed everything. It was only after they rode away in their drunkenness and stupor of depravity, that Cord was able to salvage anything from their home, and little it was, some of their firearms and ammunition, and a few personal things, but he struggled to see anything through the fire, smoke and tears.

And the brief remembrance filled his eyes with tears, remembering the bodies of his family and his struggle to see them buried and his journey since. He continued to struggle with Vengeance versus Justice, but he was determined to try the justice path and let the law do its work. He breathed deep, looked heavenward and muttered his prayer for the day and the work ahead.

The sun was bending its golden lances over the mountain behind their camp when Cord walked through the quakies, enjoying the fluttering of the aspen leaves in the morning breeze and the cool air of the mountains. Their camp was above the town, and the town was nestled in the valley at an altitude just over ten thousand feet in elevation. In the high mountains, the air was thin and those unaccustomed to the altitude often struggled with any exertion, but Cord and Tabby enjoyed the mountains and had become accustomed to the high country. He grinned when he saw Tabby sitting beside the little fire with the coffee pot dancing on the rocks as she finished the frying of the bacon and glanced at the Dutch oven baking the biscuits under the lid covered with hot coals.

"Mmmmm, smells good! And I'm hungry as a bear!" he declared as he took a seat opposite Tabby.

She looked up at him, "I bet you are, and there's enough for both of us, but come noonin', it'll be your turn to cook!" she declared. "And I'll go for a walk in the woods while you fix our food!"

"Well, I reckon fair's fair, but you might not think so after you eat my cookin'!" He chuckled as he reached for the tin plate she had dropped some bacon into.

But she held tight, "Hold on, don't you want some biscuits?"

"I do, of course I do. But where's the gravy?"

She squinted her eyes at him and lifted a biscuit as if to throw it, "You want me to hit you with this?" she growled.

Cord dropped his gaze, "Oh, I guess that means there's no gravy?"

The biscuit flattened against his forehead as he tried unsuccessfully to duck, but he grabbed it before it hit the ground and laughed as he put it on his plate. He leaned back and started to eat until Tabby said, "Hold on! Didn't you just spend time in prayer, and now you've lost all that and don't want to say thanks for our food?"

"Oh," he mumbled and bowed his head. He prayed a short prayer of thanksgiving and looked up at a smiling and laughing Tabby, who shook her head and picked up her own plate.

———

WITH THE FULL light of early morning, both Cord and Tabby were belly-down on the crest of the shoulder overlooking the valley of the Snake. Directly below them spread the hodge podge layout of Montezuma, the dozen business buildings lining the main street and the flats beyond holding scattered cabins of the many prospectors that had filed claims, some proved up on, but most now abandoned. This town was founded with the discovery of gold and for most of a decade, had prospered, but like most mountain towns, the gold had petered out, and the prospectors had disappeared with their pokes in hand. But there were still several hopeful men that dug in the dirt, washed the diggings in the waters of the Snake, and slowly filled their pokes, that were just as easily emptied in the saloons in town.

From their vantage point, Cord and Tabby could watch the roads in and out of the town. The stage road from Breckenridge coming in from the north end or mouth of the valley, the road to Coleyville climbing the timbered slope that led to the wide basin of the Saints John lode, and to the south, the road that became nothing more than a handcart trail that followed the Snake to its headwaters in a wide basin in the high country. That same road forked about a mile out of town, with the west fork following Deer Creek into another high country basin and the headwaters of Deer Creek. And on the same side of the valley, beyond a long stretch of aspen and a shallow gulley, the miner's switchback road climbed the face of the mountain they had made their temporary home.

Wherever there was access, challenging or seemingly impossible, there were men who scouted and dug prospect holes, leaving behind the holes and dumps to scar the mountainsides. But it was at those more recent diggings that the men were found full of hopes and dreams and would be possible marks for the outlaws. What Cord and Tabby were watching for was any riders, two or more in number, that were not packing prospecting tools but looking the part of outlaws eager to waylay the hopeful gold-diggers.

Cord lifted his binoculars to scan the roads and saw only one man, sourdough looking old-timer leading a loaded burro with prospect tools, walking south out of town, in no particular hurry, walking just fast enough to keep from getting stepped on by the equally ambitious burro.

Cord handed off the binoculars and let Tabby have a look-see while he shaded his eyes with his hat and hand, to scan the area with his naked eyes.

Tabby moved around, sat up with legs crossed before her and her elbows on her knees and frowned as she watched the town. She sighed heavily, lowered the binoculars and glanced to Cord, "This could get boring real quick, don'tcha think?"

"Ummhmm, but it's the best way. We can't go charging into town, guns blazing, there's too many of 'em and that would not be boring for long!"

Tabby chuckled as she handed off the binoculars. "So, how long we gonna do this?"

"However long it takes. If we're lucky, we'll catch some of 'em in groups of two, three, that will go out searching the diggings, and we can follow or..." He shrugged, chuckled, "or until our patience runs out and we come up with a better idea." Cord had rolled to his side, come up on his elbow and was looking at Tabby.

They continued their vigil until Tabby had worn her patience thin and said, "I'm gonna start puttin' things together for some lunch. How hungry are you?"

"Oh, not too, haven't done much to get hungry," mumbled Cord, still scanning the roads and trails with his binoculars. He pulled his Spencer with the telescopic sight close to his side with his free hand, but kept the binoculars focused on the trails below.

Tabby rose and walked back to the fire ring, gathering sticks and kindling on the way, and thinking about what to have for lunch. They still had some venison backstrap and she could cut some strips and hang them over the fire, and maybe she could go on a search for some yampa, osha, onions, or berries. She grinned to herself, glanced back at the prone figure of Cord and looked about as to where to start her search.

8

VISITORS

Tabby had Blue with her as she started her hunt for berries and more. The hound dog was a good companion and a watchful one as well. He had taken to Tabby right off, although his loyalty was to Cord, he liked the attention and affection given him by the woman and he had already shown his protective ways with her any time a stranger approached.

It was a warm, sunny day and the long lances of sunlight pierced the aspen grove that straddled the little spring-fed creek where Tabby searched for the berry bushes and any osha and yampa. She carried a small satchel and was quickly filling the bag as Blue sniffed most every rock and bush on the way. Blue was on the narrow game trail before Tabby and suddenly stopped, lowered his head and growled. He glanced back to Tabby, but turned back quickly to look up the game trail into the darker timber.

"What is it, boy? What do you see?" quietly asked

Tabby, coming close behind Blue and reaching out to touch his back, keeping her eyes on the trail. She heard some shuffling and huffing, smelled a dank stench, and remembered Cord talking about the smell of bear. Her eyes flared as she saw movement through the trees and she tapped Blue on his hips and said, "Let's go boy! That's a bear!" and turned to run back to their camp. Blue was beside her, often craning his head back to look at their back trail, but the rolling roar of the big bruin gave haste to their flight.

"Cord! Bear!" shouted Tabby as they neared the camp. "Bear!" she hollered, slapping aside the branches of the thick aspen as she stumbled into the clearing of their camp. Cord had come to his feet, Spencer in hand, and saw Tabby break through the trees. They had picketed the horses and mule at the edge of the aspen on the north edge of their camp, and Tabby and the bear were coming from the upper end on the east side. Cord saw the bending of the trees as the big bruin smashed through the saplings, and Tabby dived to the side by their saddles and gear.

Cord had cocked the Spencer, lifted it to his shoulder and readied himself to shoot. The wall of brown fur seemed to roll to a stop, then come erect on his hind feet, head cocked to the side and his massive mouth opening into a roar that seemed to rattle the entire mountainside. It was evident this was a sow grizzly, and probably had a cub nearby and she was being protective. Cord raised the muzzle of the rifle, readying his shot, hesitating to see what the bear would do, and watched as the monster pawed at the air and let roll another roar, followed by coughing barks. She dropped to all fours, slapping at the dirt, snapping her jaws as she growled and coughed. But when Cord did not move or make any threatening motions, the big beast snapped her jaws again, glanced to see Tabby and Blue behind the stack of gear, then turned away and ambled off into the trees.

It was a moment or two before anyone moved or spoke, listening to the retreating sounds of the big grizzly, and when silence fell on the camp, Tabby slowly rose, bag of fruit in hand and looked at Cord, letting a bashful smile paint her face, and walked to him, arms outstretched, needing a reassuring embrace.

Cord grinned, held his arms wide and accepted the woman into his arms and they held one another tightly, and slowly began to laugh as Blue rubbed against their legs. When they pulled apart, they looked at one another, tears running down Tabby's face, as she admitted, "I was so scared!"

Cord chuckled. "Me too, she was a big 'un!"

Tabby leaned back and frowned. "She?"

"Ummhmm, couldn't you tell. She's a nursing mother. Prob'ly has a cub or two back in the woods up there. Mighta heard you pickin' berries and such and came to see what was goin' on."

"Makes me want to stay outta the woods..." Tabby mumbled, leaning against Cord and holding his hand as he had his arm around her back.

"Ah, nuthin' to worry about. Now, if that had been an angry boar grizzly..." He chuckled, knowing the end of the story would have been quite different. Seldom would one shot from a Spencer .56 stop a charging grizzly, but it would make him mad. He let a slow grin split his face and asked, "Uh, did'ju find anything for lunch?"

Tabby pulled away and shook her head. "Men, all you think about is eating!"

"Oh, I don't know about that." Chuckled a grinning Cord as Tabby went to the parfleches that held the foodstuffs. As she walked back to the fire, she glanced past the reclining Cord, frowned as she looked. "What's that?" She nodded toward the town. "Riders comin' into town."

Cord rolled back and lifted his binoculars for a better look. He watched the riders, adjusted his focus and stared. He recognized the bigger of the three men, and after a moment, the others became more familiar. He spoke without moving, "Looks to be Newt Morrison, and I'm thinkin' the other two are Bill Coogan and the Mex, Yaqui." He continued watching and saw them rein up in front of the sheriff's office. Because they were on the far side, in the main road and shielded by the buildings, he lost sight of them, but he knew where they were and that told a lot, especially confirming what he suspected about Sheriff Steele.

"Things are gettin' interestin'. Maybe we'll eat an' go down to town, talk to some o' the folks."

"Thought you wanted to stay out of town, didn't you?" asked Tabby as she watched Cord come to his feet and join her at the fire.

"Just didn't want to stir things up 'fore we could cut down the odds a little. But with that bunch," nodding toward town, "we know the core of the gang is Red Legs and it's gonna take more'n just you'n me."

"WHY'RE WE STOPPIN' at the sheriff's office," whined Coogan, looking furtively from Newt to the office and back.

"Oh, thot we'd say howdy to an ol' friend," drawled Newt as he swung his leg over the cantle of his saddle to step down. "C'mon, git down an' come in, ain't nuthin' to be 'feared of," cackled Newt as he slapped the reins of his mount over the hitchrail. He stepped up on the boardwalk and pushed the door of the sheriff's office open as the two others hurried to follow. He was framed in the doorway when the sheriff looked up from his desk to see the shadowy figure of a large man outlined by the midday sun.

"What'chu want?" he growled, leaning forward on his desk. He had been sifting through the wanted posters to see if he recognized anyone, thinking especially of the one that smashed in Willy's face. When the man did not respond, Sheriff Steele came to his feet, his hand resting on the butt of his pistol as he growled again, "I said, what'chu want? If'n you ain't here fer sumpin' then git!" he waved with his free hand and started around his desk as if to rid the office of an unwanted pest.

"You raise a hand to me it'll be the last time you ever done that!" growled the shadowy figure, his thumbs hooked behind the pistol belt that hung below his paunch.

The sheriff paused, frowning, hearing what he thought was a familiar voice, then remembered, "Newt? Is that you?" he asked, doubt filling his voice. He kept his hand on the pistol and took a step closer.

Newt grinned, stepped into the office where the sun was not at his back and the sheriff broke into a grin and came closer, chuckling and slapped the newcomer on his shoulder, "Well, I was wonderin' when you'd show up!" declared Steele, sitting back on the edge of his desk. "And who's that with you?"

"You remember Coogan, an' the other'n is Yaqui, don' know if you know him," explained Newt, motioning the others into the office.

Steele shook hands with all three men, motioned them to the chairs and returned to his chair behind the desk. Newt chuckled, "Looks like you got things purty easy 'round'chere."

Steele dropped his eyes as he laughed, "Not easy,

but purty good. Got a few *'deputies'* workin' in the collectin' business, and promises from folks here-abouts of some good things to come. Only problem I got is gettin' some good men." He looked up at Newt, "Say, I had a feller in here th' other day lookin' for you and your men. Din't get his name, but he said he had some *'personal bizness'* with you, some kinda debt to pay, acted like you owed him for sumpin'."

Newt leaned forward, his hand on the edge of the desk, "What'd he look like?" he growled, anger and fear flaring in his eyes.

The reaction surprised Steele, "I thought he was a friend, thought maybe you had worked together." He paused, remembering, "Uh, lessee, he was tall, not too big, whiskers, dark eyes, wore a duster and hat, brim turned down. Had a look of meanness about him."

Newt's eyes flared, as he took a deep breath and sat back in his chair, "Ain't no friend! He's kilt some o' the men. I thot I'd killed him when I kilt that Injun squaw he was with, but he keeps comin'." He looked around the office, glancing at the two with him and back to the sheriff, "Where can I find him?"

"Dunno, think he left town. Ain't seen him around in a couple days. Had him a room o'er to the Summit Hotel, was at the Chop House when two of my men tried to take his woman and ended up dumped out back by the outhouse." He paused in his tale, mumbled to himself, "Shoulda dumped 'em *in* the outhouse."

"Kill 'em?"

"No, just smashed in the face of one, col'cocked the other'n. Fella said the woman 'bout bent the barrel of a pistol o'er his head."

The mention of a woman caught Newt's attention, "Woman? What'd she look like? Young, long brown hair, good lookin', sassy attitude?"

"Yeah, sounds like her."

Newt slowly grinned, "Yeah, yeah, been wantin' to find her. We had her for a while, used her to get to her brothers claim, but that fella with her kilt my men, took her from us, and left town in a hurry."

"We left 'fore he did," piped in Coogan, "'member?" leaning forward, lookin' at Newt.

Newt glared at his underling, shook his head, "Why'nt you two go look 'roun' town, see if you can find 'em?"

9

RECONNOITER

IT WAS MID-AFTERNOON WHEN CORD AND TABBY RODE UP behind the Summit Chop House. Cord wanted to meet with Cooky without others in the town knowing they were back. He swung down, tied Kwitcher to a post and accepted Tabby's reins to do the same for her mare, Cassi. But as soon as they turned around, Cooky came from the back door, a bucket in hand and stopped on the step. "Well, I was wonderin' if we'd be seein' you anytime soon."

Cord grinned. "We've been around, but there's others in town that we don't want to run into, so we were wonderin' if you'd have a little time to talk?"

Cooky nodded, sat the bucket down beside the stoop and sat down on the top step, elbows on his knees. "I'm listenin'." He grinned.

Cord looked around, saw a stump and a couple big rocks that had been pushed aside when the buildings rose, and motioned to the stump for Tabby, took a rock for himself and began. "Like you said, the sheriff here has no real authority. When we talked to him 'fore we left, he admitted he had been a part of the Red Legs that we've been after, but he does not know I'm huntin' 'em. I led him to believe I had some personal business with 'em, but not what he thinks." He paused and glanced to Tabby. "We've been camped up on the hill yonder, watchin', and we saw some more of the gang come into town earlier today. They went straight to the sheriff's office. I don't know what they're up to, but if it's like they did elsewhere, they're plannin' on hittin' the claims, and more, takin' what they can, killin' who they want, and more."

Cooky frowned. "Ain't there nuthin' we can do? I mean, we can't just let 'em run wild and not try to stop 'em."

"Have they come after you to take some of your business?"

"Yeah, and I put 'em off, but I'm sure they'll be back just anytime. Don't know what I can do when there's two, three, or more of 'em. I ain't much with a gun, only a fryin' pan!" He chuckled, shaking his head.

"What about other businesses, claim owners, others? Any chance of gettin' them together? When we were at Nevada City, the local folks got together and formed a Vigilante Committee and run 'em off."

"Run 'em off? Yeah, and they come here! I dunno, if I talk to some an' they ain't willin', they'd prob'ly tell the sheriff. Some folks, well, they ain't sure it's a bad thing, you know, they look at it like taxes to pay the sheriff."

"Yeah, we kinda got that idea from the woman at the hotel," responded Cord, shaking his head.

"It'd be different if we had some authority, you know, like if the sheriff from Breckenridge would come over an' run him out."

Cord grinned. "That's not about to happen. I think that sheriff would look for any excuse to stay in his office and never come out."

"You talked to him?"

"Ummhmm, and he knew nothing about Sheriff Steele. But he did say if that's what the people of the town want, it's fine with him."

"But it's not! But these folks, well, I think they'd rather just pay 'em off and not hafta worry 'bout it."

"Ummhmm, but all it takes for evil to win is for good men to do nothing!"

"I've heard that before," groaned Cooky. "If we only had some authority..." drawled the cook.

"Authority?" asked Cord.

"Yeah, you know, like if the sheriff came, or sent a deputy, or somethin' like that?"

Tabby looked at Cord, shrugged her shoulders and nodded as she motioned to Cooky. Cooky saw the motions, frowned and looked to Cord. "What?"

Cord shook his head, reached into his vest pocket and brought out his marshal's badge, "You mean like this?"

Cooky's eyes flared as he looked at the badge, up at Cord. "You mean, you're a..."

"Deputy federal marshal, yup!" Chuckled Cord, putting the badge back. He cast a glare to Tabby, then looked at Cooky. "But that's for you to know and no one else. Understand?"

"Why? If folks knew we had a marshal here, I think they'd be willing to help!"

"Usually it's the other way 'round. Most just figger it's the marshal's job, so let him do it!"

"Oh...yeah, I see what you mean," grumbled Cooky, shaking his head. "But is there *anything* you can do?"

"Maybe..." began Cord, but before he could say more, a shout came from inside the Chop House. "Hey! Anybody 'round? We're hungry!"

Cooky jumped to his feet and opened the screen door to go into the kitchen.

"Hey! Where is ever'body?" came the same voice.

Cord stood, looked through the screen and beyond into the café and saw a familiar figure standing and looking around. Cooky pushed through the swinging doors from the kitchen and answered, "Here I am, I was just takin' some trash outside. What you fellas need?" he asked. When the man turned around, Cord saw his face and recognized Yaqui. Cord moved away from the screen before he could be seen and motioned to Tabby as he spoke softly, "Let's hightail it!"

They rode north behind the business buildings,

keeping low and moving at a walk so as not to attract attention, made it to the trees that came from the flank of the big mountain to the east of the town and cut through the trees, zig-zagging back to their camp.

They stripped the horses of the gear, stacking it with the rest, and Cord returned to the point of the shoulder where they watched the doings of the valley below. Tabby followed and sat beside him. "So, what now?"

Cord had seated himself in the grass, cross-legged, and with elbows on his knees, he lifted the binoculars. As he looked, he responded, "Same as what we were doing. See what happens, what the outlaws try, maybe cut down their numbers, if we can."

"What do we look for?" asked Tabby, her frustration mounting. She wanted to strike now, she was not a patient hunter, and the memory of what these bums had done to her brothers still rankled.

"Oh, somethin' like this..." he began, motioning her alongside.

As she took a seat beside him, he handed off the binoculars. "Look to the south of town, the road yonder," he pointed.

As she lifted the field glasses, he said, "Three riders. Any look familiar?"

She watched for a moment then spoke slowly, "Yeah, the big 'un, that's the one they call Newt. He's the leader of the bunch!"

"Ummhmm, now we watch, see what they're up to, look for others. If they suspect we're here, they might try settin' a trap. So, we've got to be mighty careful."

"Why would they know we're here?"

"They talked to the sheriff, and Cooky might want to talk about a marshal in town."

"Oh," she groaned, beginning to understand Cord's preference for anonymity. "Hey, they turned on the road that goes to Coleyville."

"I wondered why Newt would be with 'em. He usually sends others to do his dirty work, but with the big mining company building that ore mill, he might be gunnin' for the big ones!"

"You think they'll give in, the company, I mean?"

"Dunno, usually an outfit like that has their own men and won't put up with much. It might give us an edge, but...if they give in, it'll just make it worse," mulled Cord. He looked down at the town, "Uh, take a look on the road goin' south, looks like two or three more riders."

"Ummhmm, looks like the sheriff, and one of the others looks like one of the Red Legs, dunno his name, but he's familiar. I've seen him before."

"Then maybe that's where we need to be," suggested Cord, rising to go to their gear and saddle the horses. As Tabby joined him, he said, "We won't get too close, don't want 'em to recognize us, but...if we can, we'll hit 'em from the trees, but only if they try to take a claim or somethin' like that." He lowered his head to look at Tabby from under his brows, giving her a *Mind your manners* glare.

"I know, I know, but..." she began.

"No buts about it. You don't go shootin' until I do, understand?"

"Oh, alright. But if you do, I will too!" she added, giving Cord her most determined stare, until they both began laughing.

10

DEER CREEK

CORD LED THE WAY, CHOOSING DIM GAME TRAILS THAT kept them in the timber and out of sight as they paralleled the riders that kept to the road beside the Snake River, always going south deeper and higher in the long valley. Whenever a break in the trees allowed, Cord and Tabby would stop and scan the far road with the binoculars, trying to keep abreast of the three men as they kept to the road that took them further up the valley. Occasionally, the riders would pass a working claim on the river, at most nodding to the prospectors but most often watched by the gold hunters who stood with rifles in hand. The road they traveled, lay at the bottom of the slope of the east-facing mountains, usually at the base of winter avalanches or rockslides that tumbled from on high in the spring or early summer melt-off. Most of the downed timber that had been claimed by winter's avalanches had been gathered and used for firewood, sluice boxes, or cabins, leaving behind a naked trough that carried runoff water in the warmer months, sometimes flooding the river and taking sluice boxes with the floods.

As the valley bent to the south and split at the confluence of Deer Creek and Snake River, the riders stayed with the Snake River, which lay in the bottom of a long, wide valley that rose toward the basin that held the headwaters of the Snake. But the trail that followed the Snake presented a problem for Cord and Tabby as it lay at the base of long talus slopes that fell from the tall mountains that cradled the valley, showing bare slopes with little or no timber to mask their presence.

Cord reined up at the edge of the timber, lifted the binoculars to look at the sheriff and his two minions. He waited a short while and when the road, which had now crossed to the east side of the river, moved into a short stretch of timber, Cord said, "Alright, let's go. We'll cross over to the other side where there's cover, and as long as we have cover, we'll follow. But if it gets where we're in the open, we'll drop back."

Tabby nodded, nudged Cassi alongside Kwitcher and sided Cord as he broke from the timber to cross over the creek that was the Snake River. The flats that held the meandering stream showed bogs, cattails, ponds and more that did little more than provide water for the grasses and wildflowers, although there were the remains of old claims, there were a few men still working the rocky terrain and apparently showing some color that kept them hard at work. The hillsides showed a few prospect holes and some that appeared to be working mines with nearby cabins, tipples for hauling up the ore buckets, and evidence of recent diggings.

Although this area had shown gold and several claims had proven up, most of the attention was now being given to silver-producing ore, usually galena and blende, some pyrite and other ore that carried silver, which had proven to be profitable, even though more difficult to extract. There had been discoveries all the way from Snake River Pass to the headwaters of the Snake and the different tribu-taries. But many of the money grubbers were intent only on gold, finding it easier to get the gold after simple panning, sluicing, or rocker boxes, for once washed, the gold was immediately available and easily picked and put in a poke, but the silver ore required milling and smelting, both costly operations.

Cord reined up, held out a hand to keep Tabby from coming alongside and he leaned forward on the pommel of his saddle, moving side to side to look through the trees into the open basin beyond. They were at the edge of the trees, a talus slope above them and a wide basin surrounded by granite-tipped mountains and cliff-edged ridges, yet in the bottom of the basin lay a little pond that held the origin spring of the river. From the cliffs on the southwest edge, fell talus slopes that ended in the greenery of the high country with blue lupine, purple locoweed, dark red tinted Icegrass, and the occasional yellow Alpine twinpod, Cord's favorite was the purple bloomed sky pilot. But the beauty of the alpine basin was broken by gunfire.

From beyond the rocky shoulder that shielded the three riders from view, staccato gunfire echoed across the basin, "Sounds like three, four shots, rifle shots'd be my guess," growled Cord. Tabby moved alongside, slipping her rifle from the scabbard, "Well?"

"Well, what?"

"Are we goin' after 'em?"

"We don't know what they're doin'! And if we go stormin' in there and all they're doin' is takin' an elk for fresh meat, we've ruined our cover and more!"

"And if we don't, they're probably killin' some sourdough prospector, stealin' his gold and more!"

"The gunfire's over. If there's any killin' we can't change it now," growled Cord, reaching down to take a rein of Tabby's mare in hand.

"If we'd stayed after 'em, we mighta stopped 'em!" pleaded Tabby.

"And maybe got ourselves killed too! Or if they'd seen us, they would've only come after us and then what?"

"Well..." sniveled the girl, frowning at Cord and slipping the rifle back in the scabbard.

Cord swung down, rifle in hand and moved to

the edge of the trees for a better look. He stood beside a big aspen, watching the trail that bent into the basin, waiting for the riders to show themselves. The binoculars hung from his neck, and when he saw movement, he dropped to one knee and lifted the binoculars. He waved Tabby close and as she neared, whispered, "I want to get a good look at these three so we'll know who they are. After they've gone, we'll go see what the shooting was about, maybe have enough on 'em to put 'em in jail."

"Now, that's more like it! Let me get a look, too!"

———

THE DIRTY CANVAS wall tent fluttered in the mountain breeze, a golden eagle circled overhead as he scouted the basin for his dinner, and the diggings of a claim beside the little stream were evident with a rocker box upended and a broken shovel alongside. The body of a man lay sprawled beside the stream, his head at the edge of the water. His canvas britches and the top of his Union suit showed dirt and blood where several bullets had pierced his back, a gold pan had been stomped on and flattened, a tethered burro had been shot and left beside the wall tent.

Cord and Tabby stepped down, going to the man and as Cord reached to roll him on his back, the man moaned, his eyes fluttered open. Cord asked, "Do you know who did this?"

"Sh...Sher...Sheriff Steele...shot me...had two

others...one ugly, other'n Mex." He choked on the words and what air remained in his bloodied lungs sputtered through the blood and the man, while held in Cord's arms, slumped in death. Cord looked to Tabby and she dropped her eyes, shaking her head as she mumbled, "I tol' ya...we shoulda..." and turned away, looking for a spade to start digging a grave.

She handed off the spade to Cord and went to the wall tent to search for something that would give the name of the claim holder. He had few personal items, one pair of canvas britches, a broken pair of galluses, a faded linen shirt, a floppy felt hat, two blankets on a crudely fashioned bunk with a bedroll atop, a water pail, frying pan, parfleche with scant rations, and little else. She sat on the three-legged stool, looking around and frowned when she saw something under the bunk. She got down on her knees, reached under the bunk and pulled out a pair of saddlebags, and noticed what appeared to be a half-buried tin plate, but she focused on the saddlebags. She rifled through the miscellaneous personal items, found a tintype of a young couple, probably him and his woman, a crumpled letter from an address in Arkansas, and a folded paper that showed a bank account in the bank at Breckenridge. Her eyebrows raised when she saw the numbers, pursed her lips and started to rise, then remembered the pie tin.

Back on her knees, she reached under the bunk, and dug around to remove the pie tin, and felt something else. She grabbed what felt like leather and pulled, bringing out a leather pouch, the type often used for gold dust, realized it was heavy and sat on the edge of the bunk to pull the drawstring pouch open to find it full of gold dust and nuggets. She chuckled, realizing the outlaws had totally missed the stash, and rose to go tell Cord.

"You gonna put a marker down?" she asked as she walked toward Cord, who was finishing covering the grave.

"You found somethin' with a name, didja?" he asked, sticking the spade in the dirt and stretching to relieve his aching back.

"Ummhmm, and more." She tossed him the gold pouch and grinned when he grunted as he caught it.

He looked at her, "Is this...?"

She nodded, "Ummhmm, and this..." holding up the deposit slip from the bank, "...says Edward Zabrisky has a lot more!"

They rode in silence as they started back to their camp, considering what might have been, and what might lay ahead for them to do, the thoughts unshared until Cord reined up, turned around in his saddle to wait for Tabby to come alongside. She stopped beside him, waiting for him to speak.

"I know you're thinkin' we shoulda gone after the men before they had a chance to hit that prospector, but..." he shook his head as he remembered, "...I haven't come this far by being careless. I've gone against these men several times before and I'm still kickin', although there were a couple times I wasn't too sure I'd make it, and now, well, with it bein' the two of us, I just don't want to be takin' unnecessary chances." He took a deep breath, shook his head slightly, "Yeah, I've thought about what happened, what we might have done an' all that, but there was no cover around there. If there had been trees and such, then we could've gotten closer, saw what was happenin' and then acted. But it was wide open!" he implored, trying to make her understand.

Tabby lowered her eyes, "Cord, I know you are tryin' to protect me, and I'm grateful, but...please, don't let that keep you, keep us, from doin' what needs to be done to stop these...these...oh, I can't even think of a word that says what I'm thinking!" she fussed, pounding her fist on the pommel.

Cord grinned, "I know how you feel, and we'll do everything we can to keep this from happening again. Let's go into town, talk to Cooky, see if anything else has happened and see what he thinks might be the best course."

Tabby sighed heavily, nodded and nudged Cassi to keep up with Kwitcher as both horses watched Blue trotting down the road before them.

11

POSSE

"WE DON'T EVEN HAVE A JAIL, CORD. THAT BACK ROOM OF the sheriff's office is just another room, no jail cells, nuthin'!" moaned Cooky, looking across the table at Cord and Tabby.

"What about the previous sheriff, what'd he do?"

"Nuthin', walked the streets, made threats, but nuthin' to him."

"I was not impressed with the sheriff in Breckenridge, but at least they have a jail. But what if..." began Cord, frowning as he thought, "what if we arrested 'em, put 'em in the back room there and had a quick trial. If they're found guilty, like they should, we'd need to hang 'em right away, but...." He paused, dropped his eyes and shook his head, "...they've got a lot o' friends around now."

Silence dropped over the trio as they reached for their coffee cups as if the answer lay in the black brew. Cooky looked at Cord, "What if you arrested 'em and took 'em to Breckenridge, put 'em in jail and let the sheriff there worry 'bout 'em?"

Cord thought a moment, "Even if we put 'em in the back room of the sheriff's office here, could we get a judge and jury together, and if we did, you think they'd stand up to Morrison and the others, find 'em guilty?"

"I don't think you could find enough people to make up a jury, much less those with enough backbone to stand up for what's right!" growled a disgruntled Cooky, shaking his head.

"Then I reckon we'll hafta take 'em to Breckenridge, put 'em in the jail there an' hope the sheriff has enough mettle to get some justice," resolved Cord. "You know anyone that'd want to help us take 'em to Breckenridge?"

"Take 'em, you ain't even got 'em arrested yet!" declared an astounded Cooky, "But it'd be the same answer as 'fore. Ain't nobody willin' to take time away from their claims and if'n they was, they'd not wanna do anything that might make trouble for 'em." He shook his head, looking around, "And if'n I din't hafta take care o' my own bizness, I'd go with, but..." he shrugged.

Cord let out a heavy breath, knowing the dilemma, but still determined to do what was right. "Well, we'll hafta parley and decide what'n when we're gonna do anything," resolved Cord, nodding to Tabby. They both stood, finished off the coffee and set down the cups, to walk out the back door to their horses.

Tabby looked at Cord, "So, whatchu thinkin'?"

"Prob'ly 'bout the same as you. We still got it to do, and we gotta start somewhere. But..." he shook his head, "I don' like puttin' you in danger."

Tabby made a face and shook her head, "Now, don't start that again. I don't wanna hafta have that conversation again!" she growled as she swung aboard Cassi, reached down and stroked the big mare's neck. She spoke to the horse, but loud enough for Cord to hear, "If he don't straighten up, I don' know what I'm gonna do! Any ideas girl, other'n kickin' him o'er the moon?"

Cord chuckled, leaned down to stroke Kwitcher's neck, "How 'bout you, boy? Think we're gonna hafta teach these newbies some manners?" Both Cord and Tabby laughed when Kwitcher started bobbing his head up and down as if agreeing with Cord.

They returned to their camp, stripped the horses and began preparing things for their supper. Cord gathered the firewood, started the little fire, filled the coffee pot with water and sat it beside the fire, all while Tabby worked at cutting some strips of back strap steak, made up a mix of sourdough for biscuits, and collected the remaining potatoes and such from their last supply jaunt, and prepared the pot for the stew. When all was on the fire, they sat back side by side on the big log, watching the fire and talking.

"You have a plan yet?" asked Tabby, already feeling a little anxious about the next day's activity.

"I'm workin' on it. The easiest will be getting the sheriff, he pretty much hangs out at his office. But the other two, don't know where or how we'll get them, less'n they show up at the office. If I try to go to the saloons to find 'em, I'm not sure about the one, I think the Mex was José Espinoza, but..." he shrugged.

"Maybe we need to just *convince* the sheriff to tell us *who* and *where* to find 'em," suggested Tabby.

"Not likely. Most outlaws don't have any good qualities, but most, probably out of fear more'n anything else, are loyal and won't give up their partners." He paused, looked back at Tabby, "But...you might have somethin' there. That'd prob'ly be our best option, all things considered. Cuz if we, me, was to go into the saloons or around town askin' questions, that'd prob'ly get back to Newt Morrison and the others and then we'd have our hands full. I'd like to get the sheriff and the two others, get 'em outta town 'fore the rest of 'em find out about it."

"Yeah, and if wishes were nuggets, we'd have enough to leave this country!" chuckled Tabby, standing to go to the fire and check the simmering supper.

————

FIRST LIGHT SHOWED Cord and Tabby riding up behind the livery, it was usually one of the earliest to open for business as most blacksmiths had a room in the big barn and were always available. As they walked into the front door, Cord spotted the blacksmith's room and started toward it, but the door opened and a burly figure emerged, stretching and yawning. He saw Cord, "What'chu want?"

"Couple things. We'd like to put our horses up for a short while, and ask a question or two."

"Bring 'em in, there's empty stalls yonder," he nodded toward the darkened interior. Cord grinned, motioned to Tabby to get the horses, then asked, "Yesterday, the sheriff and two of his men left town, came back late afternoon. Could you tell me who he had with him? One of 'em was a Mex, the other'n a skinny fella."

"Dunno for sure. Ain't seen the one b'fore, but the skinny one was Harold Newsome, short, skinny, mousy type. He's been aroun' a while, tried pannin' but din't know what he was doin' and the sheriff put him to work. The Mex, I think sheriff called him Jośe."

"Their horses here?" asked Cord.

"Ummhmm, they're back there."

"Well, if my partner," nodding to Tabby, who had her duster collar turned up and her hat brim down to hide her face a little, "comes back in and wants those horses and the sheriff's, saddled and ready to go, you do that won't you?"

"Why should I do what you want?" moaned the burly man, tucking his thumbs under his galluses and scowling at Cord.

Cord pulled out his badge, held it in his palm and showed the blacksmith, who looked with wide eyes and an open mouth, before looking up at Cord. "You gonna arrest 'em?"

"Maybe, but don't you say anything, or I'll hafta arrest you too!"

The blacksmith stepped back a step and held both hands out, palms up, "Oh, don' worry 'bout me! I ain't sayin' nuthin' to nobody!"

"Good, we'll count on that."

With a nod to Tabby, they left the livery, heading toward the sheriff's office. But the office was locked and dark. Cord suggested, "Prob'ly havin' breakfast at Cooky's. Let's go there, an' if it ain't crowded, we'll have breakfast, meet him back to the office after."

"You sure?"

"Ummhmm, but we'll try to keep you *incognito*," he chuckled.

Tabby laughed, "Well, listen to you, usin' them big words and such!"

When they entered the restaurant, they spotted the sheriff at a table with one other, and the look of the other man seemed to match the description they had of the second skinny and ugly man. Cord chuckled as he nudged Tabby toward another table. The sheriff spotted them, grinned and nodded, and Cord returned the same. When Cooky came to their table with a fresh pot of coffee, he turned his back to the sheriff and poured the coffee as he asked, "You're riskin' things a little, ain'tchu?"

"Nah, we'll be fine," responded Cord, lifting his cup for Cooky to fill.

When the sheriff and his minion rose to leave, he walked by Cord's table, and Cord spoke softly, "Uh, we'll be over shortly. You forgot something yesterday."

The sheriff paused and looked at Cord, frowned, "What'd I forget?"

Cord frowned, looking around the restaurant, and whispered, "Not here! Later!"

When Cord and Tabby stepped inside the sheriff's office, they were greeted by frowns and grunts from the sheriff and the one known as Harold. Cord motioned for Tabby to take a chair to his right, Harold was against the wall on the left, and Cord stepped before the desk and stood in front of the sheriff. He pulled out the gold pouch from the claim and plopped it on the desk, "You forgot something from Zabrisky's claim yesterday!"

The sheriff frowned, looked up at Cord and pulled his chair closer to the desk and reached for the pouch. He pulled the drawstrings to open the pouch, and poured out some of the contents. The sudden rush of gold dust and nuggets brought both Harold and the sheriff to their feet to reach for the raw gold, but Cord put his hand atop the pile.

The sheriff growled at Harold, "I tol' you idjits! There had to be more, but no..."

Cord chuckled, looked to the startled Harold and said, "How 'bout you goin' to get José so we can split this up 'tween us. But don't say anything to anybody else, otherwise you'll hafta share with all the others. You don' wanna to that, do ya?"

Harold looked from Cord to the sheriff who was grinning and nodding, and Harold turned and quickly left. The sheriff looked at Cord, "How'dju know?"

"Oh, we saw you on the trail, wondered about it, so we followed you a ways. After you left, we went to the diggin's and looked around. Found that under the ol' man's bunk," chuckled Cord, "Your helpers ain't too good at their chosen occupation. Maybe you better give 'em some teachin'!" offered Cord, pulling a chair close to the desk to seat himself between the sheriff and his view of Tabby. He looked around the office, saw some coat pegs on the far wall, but only one had a coat, two of the others held sets of shackles, although there was enough dust on them, there was no mistaking they had never been used. He grinned, reached inside his duster and pulled out his Colt, aiming it at the sheriff, "So, for now, we're goin' to take care of things."

"What're you doin'?" growled the sheriff.

"Arresting you," stated Cord, standing and motioning with his pistol for the sheriff to rise, "An' don'tchu even think about using your pistol," he ordered, bringing his Colt to full cock. "Turn around," he ordered and motioned for Tabby to put the shackles on the sheriff's wrists. Once done, he shoved the sheriff into the back room, to be seated on the bench. He checked the back door, made certain it was secured and locked, then started out the door to the outer office. He glanced to the sheriff, "Don't worry, Sheriff, it'll all be over soon."

"Yeah, you're right about that, an' when they get'chu, I'm gonna put the rope aroun' yore neck!" growled the sheriff. Cord just grinned, stuffed a neckerchief in the sheriff's mouth and shut the door.

He motioned Tabby to her chair, and he seated himself behind the desk. They were no sooner seated than the door slapped open, and the two men stormed inside. Harold went to the desk, turned to Jośe and said, "See! Tol'ja! An' it's ours, all ours!"

When he looked up at Cord, he was staring into the black hole of the muzzle of the Colt in Cord's hands. Cord grinned, said, "Now, just stand still, put your hands behind your back."

"Wha'chu doin'? whined Harold, glancing from Cord to Jośe and back.

"Do it!" ordered Cord, "Carefully!" he added. Both men put their hands behind their back, glaring at Cord as he came around the desk and removed their pistols and a knife from a sheath in Jośe's belt. As he stepped back, Tabby put the shackles on the two men, and Cord ordered them to sit on the floor, facing the outer wall. "Bring the horses around, we'll be out back." With a nod, Tabby left, keeping her collar up, brim down, and head tucked into the collar of her duster.

12

ESCORT

CORD LED OUT WITH THE THREE PRISONERS, STILL shackled but on their own horses, following close behind. Cord had used a common rope from his saddle to each of the horses, all tethered together, and him leading the pack. Tabby followed behind and both Cord and Tabby had a coach gun shotgun, double-barreled 12 gauge, resting on the pommels of their saddles.

They rode behind the business buildings, taking a little used trail that was cut before the town had grown, and had followed the east bank of the river. This kept them from view from the middle of town, but not totally obscured. As they passed the last of the buildings, they soon entered the scattered trees between the stage road and the river. Once out of town and as the trees thinned, they took to the stage road. The prisoners still had shackles on their wrists behind their back, and Cord had also tied their feet to the stirrups with rope, ensuring they would not try to jump from the saddles and make a getaway into the trees or wherever. But the restraints elicited considerable complaining from the three.

"Hey, can you loosen these cuffs, they're all fired tight an' hurtin'!" shouted Harold, the skinny complainer.

"Sure, we'll loosen them when we get to Brecken-ridge!" retorted Cord.

———

"You won't b'lieve what I just seen!" declared Willy Sherman as he waddled into the restaurant where the rest of the men were gathered around two tables, downing their breakfast.

"Well?" growled Newt Morrison, pausing for just a moment as he stuffed his face with the biscuits and gravy.

"What'chu mean, well?" whined Sherman. "You're gonna spit that out when I tell ya!"

"You better talk, an' quick, 'fore I throttle you!" growled Morrison, glaring at the only man who was bigger and fatter than him.

He pulled out an empty chair from the second table, sat down and hollered at the woman who was waiting tables, "Hey! Bring me some breakfast, I don't care what it is, just make sure there's plenty!" He laughed as he turned around and scooted closer to the table, those that sat at his table were mostly men that had been with the sheriff. Morrison and his men were at the other table.

Morrison growled, "You better start talkin' or you won't be eatin' no breakfast!"

"Yeah, yeah, well, I was comin' from the cabin and saw some riders. Thought it was a little early for you'ns to be out an' about, cuz we're the onliest ones that go in a bunch anywhere, an' there was five of 'em. But sumpin' was different, so I stepped to the corner of the outhouse, you know, the one there by the trail b'low the cabin. An' sure 'nuff, there was five of 'em, but three of 'em was all tied up, hands behind their back an' such, an' there was a fella in a duster out front with a shotgun o'er his pommel, and another'n, but littler, behind 'em, also in a duster and with a shotgun."

"So, who were they?" asked Morrison.

"That's the best part. You'll never guess who they was!" He cackled, turning his attention to the woman bringing his plate of biscuits, gravy, eggs, bacon, potatoes, and more. He leaned back to let her set the plate down, rubbing his hands together and looking at the food. "Mmmm, smells good!" and reached for his knife and fork to dig in, but stopped when a growl came from the other table accompanied by the scraping of a chair.

Morrison came around the table, glaring at the oversized Willy Sherman who was focused on his food, but his attention was arrested when he felt the barrel of the Remington in Morrison's hand pressed against his head and heard the click of the cocking hammer.

Sherman froze in place, afraid to move or speak, until Morrison growled, "Talk!"

"Alright, alright. The three in the middle was Sheriff Steele, and the others were Harold Newsome and that Mex that come with you, Jose."

"What'd you say?" growled Morrison, although he heard the report quite well, but did not believe what he heard.

"I said..."

"I know what you said. Where they goin'?"

"I dunno, they's just goin'..." shrugged the fat man, ogling his plate of food, anxious to put it away.

One of the men from Newt's table spoke up, "If they was in shackles, prob'ly arrested and goin' to Breckenridge." It was the narrow-faced, whiskery, marmot-looking Buck Smithers, that gave his opinion.

Newt glared at him, "Don'chu think I know that? But who has the authority to arrest the sheriff?" He was met with silence from both tables, none venturing a guess and no one having the mental capacity to solve the problem. "If they do any talkin' we could be in a puddle of trouble. We need to get 'em back." He grumbled a little, looked back at Willy Sherman, who was stuffing his face, "You said there was two of 'em?"

Willy nodded his head, his mouth full as he mumbled something unintelligible.

Newt Morrison was ever the wily one and would not risk his own hide, but would send others. He looked around at the men, "Coogan! You take Pence an' Parker there. Git goin' an' overtake 'em. Three of you oughta get the two o' them easy."

The men were slow to rise and Newt growled, "NOW!!" and the three men came to their feet, two with coffee cups in hand, taking a last swig of the black brew. Coogan motioned for them to get a move on, and the three hustled out the door to the mumbles, grumbles, and gripes of Morrison.

As they walked to the livery for their horses, Coogan looked at the others, "The way I see it, fellas, is we get them three back, or we just keep goin' an' never come back to this country. You with me?" Coogan was new to the others, but he was one of the original Jayhawkers. A bulbous nose and patchy whiskers did little for his appearance, but his reputation was well-founded as a back shooter and throat cutter. The two newer men had their own reputations as Parker was just shy of six feet, with thick wavy hair and broad shoulders. He was a quiet man that everyone seemed to steer clear of, but the second man was spooky in his own right. He was a known gunman, with killer's eyes that struck fear in anyone, especially when he was handling his razor-sharp knives, for he always had at least two knives in sheaths at his belt, but most thought he had at least two more hidden. Yet they yielded to the leadership of Coogan and all three hustled for their horses and were soon on the trail, leaving town at a gallop, kicking rocks and dust up behind them.

————

THE STAGE ROAD between Montezuma and Breckenridge hugged the flanks of the mountains and the edge of the timber as it followed the Snake River west. The road stretched out a little over fifteen miles, and Cord had expected it to take most of the day with a need of stopping about midday for the horses to have a breather, and maybe feed the prisoners and themselves.

The road followed the river through the deep gorge of the Snake, but after about five miles, the mouth of the gorge opened to the confluence with the North Fork of the Snake River. From there the valley widened with talus slopes on the north with scattered timber on the high ridges, while the broad shoulders on the south rose with thick black timber. They pushed on, with the prisoners continually grumbling and moaning their discomfort but receiving no sympathy from their captors. When they came to the confluence with Soda Creek and the road and river dropped into a steep-walled canyon, they stopped. Choosing a bit of a clearing in the thick timber on the left side of the road, Cord told Tabby, "You get down first, I'll keep the coach gun coverin' 'em while you get down, then you can cover 'em while I slide off."

Tabby gladly slid to the ground, stepped back away from her big mare and cradled the coach gun in the crook of her left arm, her right hand on the grip, thumb on the hammers and finger on the triggers. She showed a sardonic grin as the first of the outlaws, the sheriff, had his feet untied, and Cord helped him to the ground. The sheriff almost fell, staggered against Cord, but the cocking of the hammers sounded loud and gave the sheriff pause. Cord stepped away and pushed the sheriff toward the creek bank, "Sit! I'll undo you in a minute to let you get a drink."

Cord finished getting the three off their mounts, released one hand and put that shackle on one leg, but it gave the men the freedom to belly down and get some water from the creek. When their thirst was slaked, Cord separated them, allowing each one a separate tree to sit against after he gave them some jerky. After Cord and Tabby had watered the animals, loosened the cinches and let them graze on the creek banks, they alternated standing guard, but when the men started making remarks about Tabby, for they had discovered she was a woman when she spoke and shed her duster, Cord stepped forward, "We'll have none of that!"

Steele snarled, "So, what'chu gonna do? Shoot us fer talkin' to the woman?"

"No, I won't, but she might!" He chuckled. He nodded to Tabby and she took that as permission and she blasted one barrel of the coach gun into the

branches above the two with the sheriff, making all
of them jerk in shock, as the blast echoed across the
canyon, multiplying the roar. When the branches,
bark, and more tumbled down on their heads, they
scrunched up their shoulders, trying to keep the
debris from going down their necks and scooted
away from the trees, looking like hobbled
jackrabbits.

Cord and Tabby both laughed, and Cord looked
at the men, "Tol'ja!" He stepped back, motioned to
the men with a wave of his shotgun and ordered,
"Let's get mounted. Tabby, you watch 'em, I'll
tighten the cinches and such, and we'll get 'em
mounted one at a time." He looked at the men, "You,
Jośe, c'mere."

It was awkward, but when the prisoners
mounted, they still had one hand shackled to one
ankle. But with a free hand they could swing aboard,
and then Cord would release the ankle shackle, put it
on the other wrist keeping their hands behind them.
He would then use the rope to tie one ankle to the
other with the rope passing under the belly of the
mount. To keep them in place, Cord looped the reins
of both horses together, then turned to the third.

The mounting of the first two went without any
problem, but when Sheriff Steele swung aboard and
Cord reached for the shackle, he loosed the shackle
and started to put it on the free hand, but the sheriff
kicked out, knocking Cord back, but Cord kept the
shackle in hand and when the sheriff kicked his

horse, the horse left without him and he came off with a crash flat of his back with the shackle still in Cord's hand.

Cord quickly rolled away from the man, came to his feet, and looked down at a semi-conscious sheriff. "Alright, if that's the way you want it," he growled, and rolled the sheriff onto his belly, locked the shackles together behind his back, and went for the sheriff's horse that was standing at the edge of the stream, grazing contentedly on some grass. Cord led the horse back to where the sheriff lay, glanced at the others as they sat on their mounts, and ground tied the horse, then grabbed the sheriff and dragged his body over the saddle, belly down, and tied his feet with the rope, running the loose end under the belly of the horse and wrapped it around the neck of the sheriff.

Tabby said, "Ain't that kinda dangerous?"

"Not for us," drawled Cord, lifting his shotgun to guard the others while Tabby mounted. Once aboard, he handed her coach gun to her, mounted Kwitcher and with a wave to Blue, they started back on the road.

13

CONFRONTATION

"HEY COOGAN! I KNOW THIS ROAD, AN' IF WE CUT ACROSS this flat an' Soda Creek, we can take that bit of a saddle and drop to the other side by way of Soda Gulch!" declared Perry Parker, one of the sheriff's men who had been around Montezuma for a couple years.

"Will that get us ahead of 'em?" growled Coogan, knowing this was country that the men of Sheriff Steele knew better than him an' those that rode with Morrison.

"Yeah, it should. We might hafta push 'em a little, but we should get there 'fore they do. This road they're followin' is the stage road an' it follows the Snake till it meets up with the Blue River, then the stage road follows the Blue up to Breckenridge, if'n that's where they're goin'!" explained Pence, glancing to a nodding Parker.

Coogan noticed the response of the two men,

looking at one another in agreement, and since he was a stranger in these parts, he thought it would be best to go with them. He nodded, "Let's do it! You lead out, Pence!" They had been on the trail of the sheriff and his captors, not certain as to who they were, but they had been far enough behind to keep out of sight, although not by any intentional planning of Coogan. By the tracks they had been gaining on them a little, but since they stopped for noonin' and Coogan and his men did not, they were coming up closer behind them, but wanted to get ahead before trying to take them. Coogan chuckled, shaking his head slowly, thinking. *And if we can't take 'em, it'd be best to keep right on goin' cuz Newt won' be happy a'tall!*

———

"WHEN YOU THINK we'll get to Breckenridge?" asked Tabby, looking around at the steep-walled canyon of the Snake River.

"Oh, late afternoon, I reckon, dependin'..." responded Cord.

"Dependin'?"

"I'm guessin' that word has gotten out about the missin' sheriff, and maybe some of his cohorts might come lookin' for him. If so, an' if they catch up with us, they might try to *delay* us a little," laughed Cord. He was in the lead and had to twist around in his saddle to talk with Tabby, the talk passing over the two captives, Harold Newsome and Jośe Espinoza, eliciting mumbled comments from both. The sheriff was still belly-down and probably unconscious, for he had not begun to complain yet, although he was expected to voice his discomfort.

"So," continued Cord, "make sure you're covered, and keep your coach gun on those three. I'll do the same, dunno if they'll get out front of us, but maybe. Whichever one of us is facin' 'em when they come, the other'n will guard the prisoners, and don't hesitate to give them a *shotgun trial* if they need it."

"Gotcha! And...I like the sound of that!"

"Of what?"

"Shotgun Trial, ummhumm..." she grinned as she waved the double-barreled coach gun at the prisoners who had twisted around in their saddles to look her way.

The stage road hugged the flanks of the south face of the canyon until it opened near the mouth of the Snake and the confluence with the Blue. It bent around the point of the low hills coming from the south and siding the Blue, then hugged the east bank of the Blue River as it started south toward Breckenridge. Although the Blue was in the bottom of a valley, it was not a canyon like that of the Snake, a wider bottom offered several stretches of the stage road that was wide open and uncovered by any trees. The flanks of the hills showed sparse juniper and piñon above the road, rocky shoulders close in, and the trail was dry and dusty.

Everyone was getting tired, cranky and dirty, and the complaints flowed easily, especially when the sheriff gained consciousness and started squirming, kicking, cussing and more. His carrying on had distracted Cord who reined up and turned back to face the three led horses bearing the prisoners, but the sudden clatter of hooves on the road behind him instantly brought him around to face the three riders coming toward them. Cord knew these were henchmen of Morrison, and he turned Kwitcher across the road, facing the oncoming trio with his left side and the muzzle of the double-barreled coach gun. They reined up, raising a dust cloud, but sat side by side, hands on the butts of their pistols still in the holsters.

Coogan pushed forward a couple steps, stopped and lifted his right hand, "Now, hold on there! No reason to get jumpy. Just let them three go and you an' yore partner just ride on, and ain't nobody gettin' shot. What say?"

Cord had watched the three and made a quick judgment. The man on the left had black eyes that Cord thought were killer's eyes and he did not waver as he looked at those before him. The other man on the far side of the talker was a solid-looking character, and no fear showed on his face. The talker was just that, more of a talker than a fighter. Cord knew what he would do, and who to take first, if needed.

He spoke up in response to the challenge, "I say you might want to take a closer look. If you can see past the end of that nose of yours, you can see my partner has a coach gun just like mine, but it's pointed at the prisoners. While mine is pointed right at your middle. Now..." paused Cord, chuckling, "if you prefer, we'll give these three, and you three, what we call a *shotgun trial*, seein' as how you're already showin' how guilty you are."

"What'chu mean?" growled Coogan, scowling at Cord, his wrinkled brow bringing the brim of his hat down to shade his dancing black eyes and whiskery face.

Cord interpreted his expression as one of confusion and fear. "Just what you think it means, now..." Cord began but was interrupted by the belly-down sheriff, who grunted as he tried to holler.

"Either kill 'em or shut up an' get outta the way!" shouted the sheriff. As he did, the two behind Coogan went for their pistols, but the coach gun roared, first one barrel and then the other, but the blasts were so close together and the cloud of smoke from the barrels so thick, it seemed like one thunderous roar.

At the first move, the two prisoners dug heels to their mounts, but the leads were wrapped around the horn of Cord's saddle and the horses kicked off to the side, making the body of the sheriff slide to the side, his head almost under the belly of the horse. When the two outlaws tried their move, Tabby dropped the hammers on her coach gun, the first blast taking Harold Newsome in his chest, neck, and shoulder, driving him off his mount to hang upside down on the far side. The second blast splattered the left shoulder, chest, neck and face of Jośe Espinoza.

As the horses fought against their leads and the last prisoner was the sheriff belly down, Tabby rested the coach gun between her and the pommel as she pulled the Colt from the holster and aimed it at the back of the head of the sheriff, hesitant to pull the trigger for fear of hitting the horse in the belly.

Cord's coach gun emptied the two saddles of Pence and Parker, and in the smoke, Coogan pulled his pistol, but the smoke from the shotgun obscured Cord and prompted Coogan to shoot blindly through the grey cloud. But the smoke hung long enough for Cord to slip his Colt from the holster and drop the hammer on Coogan, twice, emptying his saddle.

With the shooting ended, the horses began to settle down and Cord looked around, saw the bodies of the three outlaws on the ground, unmoving, then looked back at the horses that still milled about behind him, their leads still wrapped around his pommel. He saw the two empty saddles, bodies on the ground, and the bent legs of the sheriff as he hung belly-down over his mount, but he was not dead as he tried kicking free, but failing, and not for lack of cursing and growling threats. He looked for Tabby, saw her empty saddle and quickly dropped to the ground and ran back to where the sorrel mare, Cassi, stood, restlessly sidestepping, avoiding the mounts of the outlaws. Lying in a heap on the ground was the bloody duster of Tabby and the form was unmoving.

He dropped to one knee beside her, gently rolled her to her back, "Tabby, Tabby..." he mumbled, looking her over. Her eyes were pinched shut, but she was breathing in gasps. He pulled open her duster, saw blood just above the belt on her right side. He opened the coat wider, saw no other wounds, tugged the shirt free, and looked at the wound. The bullet, apparently one of the wild shots from Coogan, had cut a trench through her side, deep and black, and bleeding, but nothing more than a flesh wound. She coughed, took a deep breath and looked at Cord, "What're you doin'?" she asked, frowning at Cord and trying to look at her wound.

"You need doctorin'. We're goin' into Breckenridge, find a doctor."

"What about them?"

"Only one left...the sheriff," growled Cord, sitting back on his heels, "an he ain't none too happy. He's still hangin' upside down."

"Go tend to him, I'll be alright. Then you can help me back on Cassi an' we'll go. But wait, aren't you gonna bury them?" nodding toward the outlaws.

"Dunno. I'll look aroun' for some place to dump 'em, if not, we'll just put 'em on their horses an' take 'em into town," he shrugged.

14

BRECKENRIDGE

CORD QUICKLY BANDAGED THE WOUND ON TABBY'S SIDE, propped her up against a big rock and went about getting the sheriff upright on his saddle, and with the horse tethered and the sheriff shackled, he loaded each of the bodies on the horses, lined them out two-by-two with leads attached to the saddle of the horse in front of it, and soon had a caravan of sorts with Cord taking the lead, six horses with five bodies and the sheriff, and Tabby bringing up the rear. Tabby had reassured Cord she was alright and could make it, and once in the saddle with the reloaded coach gun laying across the pommel, she was behind the sheriff and explained to him, "If you do anything, and I mean anything, I'm gonna enjoy blowing you right out of that saddle and all the way to kingdom come, just like I did them other two!" The sheriff, head hanging and struggling to breathe because of apparent broken ribs after his belly-down ride, just shook his head and mumbled.

When they rode into Breckenridge, people stopped and stared, many followed, as the long line of bodies was a sight that caught everyone's attention. Many stood on the boardwalk, pointing, talking, the few women with mouths agape but hands over their lower faces, and men nudging one another and all asking questions. The more curious and bold ones stepped into the street to follow as the strange entourage made its way to the sheriff's office.

When they stopped in front of the office, Cord swung down, stepped up on the boardwalk and pushed into the sheriff's sanctum. The sheriff and Cord soon appeared on the boardwalk, with the sheriff frowning, looking at the strange sight, and pushed his hat back as he scratched his head, looking from the horses and their baggage, to Cord, until Tabby hollered, "How 'bout gettin' this'n off an' inside. I need to go see the doc!"

The sheriff looked at Cord, back to the bodies and both men stepped back inside the office. The sheriff, as he walked behind his desk, "I got all these warrants an' such from the office of Marshal Shaffenberg, but I din't know you was the local deputy marshal, so..." he shrugged, as he handed the stack of papers to Cord.

"Well, Sheriff, I reckon there's warrants here on all of these men, especially the former sheriff of Montezuma, Byron Steele, some of the others, I don't know their names, but a couple of 'em, are named here, Bill Coogan and Jośe Espinoza. The others will fill some of the no-name warrants, as two of 'em were with Coogan when they jumped us, and one was with Steele and Espinoza when they killed Zabrisky and stole his poke."

The sheriff nodded, started to the door, and once outside, looked around at the crowd and called out to two of the men, "You, Lindsey and Modine, you men take these dead'uns o'er to the undertaker Ames, an' take the horses to the livery!" As the sheriff watched his men take the horses and bodies, Cord went to fetch the former Sheriff Steele, untying his feet from the stirrups and pulling him off his saddle, then with a hand on Steele's elbow, he marched the shackled former sheriff into the office and into a jail cell. Once inside, Cord removed the shackles and let the sheriff drop to the bunk, grumbling and cursing all the while.

Sheriff Packer said, "I'll talk to the judge, see if we can get a trial set for tomorrow an' get this o'er with. You an' your deputy will need to testify an' such, but won't take long."

"That's good. We need to get back to Montezuma 'fore the others hightail it outta there."

"You mean those?" nodding to the remaining warrants in Cord's hand.

"And others. These have a way of adding new recruits all the time. Reckon there's plenty of wannabe miners that found out mining was work and they weren't gettin' somethin' for nothin' and..." he chuckled.

"We've had that here too, but I usually *encourage* them to get honest work, and there's plenty of that around, what with the new discoveries of silver, or I show 'em the way outta town. Keeps things peaceable that way," he chuckled.

Cord nodded, "We need to get Tabby to the doctor, where'bouts will we find him?"

The sheriff frowned, "Tabby? Your deputy is a woman?"

"And a mighty good one. But she took a bullet when they hit us, and she needs tendin' to..."

The sheriff nodded, "Uh, yeah, his office is at his house, down near the end of Main Street, got a white sign out."

"Thanks Sheriff," nodded Cord and turned to leave.

He swung aboard Kwitcher and with Tabby at his side, they rode to the far end of Main Street, saw the sign and stopped. Cord swung down, helped Tabby down as she winced and bit her lip to keep from crying out, and helped her to the door. The door was answered by a woman, who frowned, looking from Cord to Tabby and asked, "What do you need?" with a disapproving frown on her face.

"Ma'am, she," nodding to Tabby as he held her up with an arm around her waist, "was hit with a bullet, in the side, and we'd like the doctor to take a look."

"Oh, yes, certainly," she exclaimed, replacing the frown with a compassionate expression as she looked at Tabby, reaching out to help her inside. She was ushered into the office, and the woman helped her remove the duster, hat, and helped her to the exam table, with several frowns directed at Cord.

When the doctor finished, he stepped back, looked at Cord and asked, "How'd that happen?"

"We were bringing some prisoners into town, and before we got here, some of their gang hit us, trying to take them from us. She took a stray bullet that was meant for me."

"The sheriff know about this," scowled the doctor.

"We delivered the only live prisoner and the dead ones to him just before we came here."

"How is it that you were bringing in prisoners?"

"I'm a deputy federal marshal."

The doctor and his wife both stepped back, their frowns of disapproval changing to curious stares.

"Are we done?" asked Tabby, pulling herself together, fussing with the shirt and reaching for her duster.

"Yes, but you'll need to change that bandage," stated the doctor, nodding to his wife who turned to their cabinets and retrieved some additional bandages and more. She handed it off to the doctor who held it out to Tabby, "This will do for the first couple changes, then use your own judgment on how it's mending."

Tabby nodded, accepting the small bundle and slid off the exam table. Cord offered to pay the doctor but it was refused, "No, no, you've already done enough for this part of the county by bringing in those outlaws. We need more folks like you." He reached out to shake hands with Cord and Tabby, smiling broadly as his wife stood at his side.

They rode their horses toward the other end of town, stopping at the livery to put them away. After putting them in a stall, giving them a brief rub down and stacking their gear, they walked the short distance to the bank. Both Cord and Tabby went inside, were greeted by a mousy man sitting behind a desk near the front door, "Good afternoon, may I help you?"

"Yes, we'd like to talk to the boss man," stated Cord, looking around the bank.

"Uh," began the weasel-looking man as he scowled at Cord, "what is it you need? Perhaps I can help you."

"No, it's about the account of a dead miner and a considerable amount of gold, we need to talk to the man in charge," stated Cord, stoically glaring at the speaker.

The underling rose, twisted his way to the office door with the name of the banker, *Reuben Forsyth, President*, in gold on the frosted window, rapped on the door and entered.

He quickly returned, looked up at Cord and said, "Follow me, please."

When Cord and Tabby entered the office, they both doffed their hats and the banker did a double-take when the long hair of Tabby fell over her collar. She smiled as she sat down, a muffled chuckle at the response of the banker, and let Cord begin their business.

"Mr. Forsyth, I'm Cordell Beckett, deputy marshal, and this," he began, setting the heavy pouch of gold on the banker's desk, "is gold from the claim of Edward Zabrisky, and this," placing the paperwork showing the Zabrisky account, "shows that Mr. Zabrisky has an account here. We want you to deposit this," tapping the bag of gold, "into his account and contact his wife for instructions as to its disposition. This," he placed a letter beside the account ledger, "tells of her name and address."

The banker frowned, "And where is Mr. Zabrisky?"

"He was killed by some men, including one that was turned over to Sheriff Packer, he will arrange a trial for him."

"I see. And how much gold is there?"

"About six to seven pounds. I would like you to measure it out before we leave, please."

The banker frowned, not appreciating the implication of impropriety by his request to witness the measuring, but he nodded, motioning to the mousy assistant who left and soon returned with a scale and accessories for measuring the gold. When it was finished, the clerk turned to Forsyth and declared,

"Exactly six and one-quarter pounds, or one hundred ounces, at today's prices of twenty-seven dollars per ounce, that is twenty-seven hundred dollars exactly."

"Very good Hortense, that will be all," drawled the banker, dismissing the clerk. He looked at Cord, "I will contact Mrs. Zabrisky right away and we will do as she requires. Will that be all?"

"For now, yes. But we might be doing additional business in the future," offered Cord, rising and holding a hand out for Tabby. They quietly left the bank and Tabby asked, "Should we go to the stage office to send a letter to Mrs. Zabrisky?"

Cord chuckled, "That's exactly what we need to do. I want her to get our letter before the banker's."

15

RETURN

"So, that's what justice feels like, huh?" drawled Tabby. She was leaning forward on the pommel of her saddle as she looked over at Cord. It was late morning and they had ridden from Breckenridge after the trial of the former sheriff was completed.

"Well, yeah, I reckon," answered Cord. "According to the sheriff, it'll take a while for them to carry it out, what with building the gallows and such. Might have a hard time finding enough timber to build one, but..." he shrugged.

"I think our shotgun trial was better," stated Tabby. "I don't like shootin' men, but..."

"Ummhmm, I know what'chu mean," agreed Cord, shaking his head and taking in a deep breath that lifted his shoulders as he turned to look at Tabby.

"So, now what?" asked Tabby. They were headed back to Montezuma, and she had assumed they

would continue their hunt for the rest of the Red
Legs that had killed her brothers.

"Depends on what we find at Montezuma. The
rest of the outlaws are still there, and three of 'em
were sent out after us. No tellin' what they'll do
when they hear about the trial and the sheriff getting
sentenced to hang."

"They won't try anything, will they?"

"You mean about Steele?"

"Yeah, I mean, they won't try to get him out 'fore
the hangin', will they?"

"Never know about them. But what little I know
about Newt Morrison, he might just think he's the
new leader of the whole bunch and he might even try
makin' himself the new sheriff."

"Nooo..." stated Tabby, shaking her head. "The
town won't stand for that, will they?"

"Just hafta wait an' see!"

They rode in silence for a short distance until
Tabby spoke up again, "I had to laugh when Steele
tried to accuse you of stealin' the gold, sayin' you
was the one that killed Zabrisky for the gold. When
the banker explained what we done, that kinda fixed
him. I looked at him when the banker said that, and
he hung his head, knowing he was done for," she
grinned.

"Those that get in positions of power, often use
that power for their own gain. He took that position
upon himself and used it, and when no one stood
against him, he thought he could get away with

anything. But...the truth eventually came out. It's just too bad that sometimes it takes a long time for evil to get its rightful due."

"And sometimes, when good people do nothing, evil wins!" declared Tabby.

"Not always, we can't think like that. My pa used to always remind me that God is always triumphant, just like when Jesus went to the cross. The evil crowd thought they won, but three days later, Jesus came forth and His triumph was declared. It's because of His triumph, that we can be forgiven of our sin and live in victory. But...he never said it would be easy, and he did say we could have the victory. My Pa made me memorize a couple verses to that effect. *But thanks be to God, which giveth us the victory through the Lord Jesus Christ. Therefore, my beloved brethren, be ye stedfast, unmoveable, always abounding in the work of the Lord, forasmuch as ye know that your labour is not in vain in the Lord.* (I Corinthians 15:57-58)"

"Well, we'll just hafta wait an' see. There's still a bunch of 'em back to Montezuma!" declared Tabby, glancing sidelong at Cord.

"I ain't seen none of 'em! Not since you left, well, maybe the day after you left," drawled Cooky, pouring their coffee as they sat at the table by the window.

"Well, that don't mean they left, does it?" responded Cord, lifting his steaming cup for a sip of the hot brew.

"I don't know what it means, but it suits me

if'n they did leave! They was gettin' all-fired onery 'round'chere! Fights in the saloons, on the street, even in here! Looky there," he pointed to the corner where a stack of broken chairs and tables sat askew. "They done that! Wouldn't pay for it neither!" He harumphed as he stomped away to the kitchen.

"You think they left?" asked Tabby, sounding disappointed, frowning into her cup.

"Dunno, reckon we'll find out."

THEY RETURNED to their camp on the shoulder of the mountain overlooking Montezuma. The mule had been picketed within reach of both water and graze and stood looking at them with an expression that could be interpreted as just about anything, seeing as how he was a recalcitrant mule. Once the animals were tended to, Cord took the binoculars and his Spencer to his promontory to watch the town and the comings and goings, still wondering about Newt Morrison and the rest of the Red Legs. Although he knew they were no longer associated with the wartime Red Legs and that many of the men had never been a part, he still identified them as such whenever he spoke about them or thought about them. The memory of what happened to his family was forever burned into his memory, and it took very little to bring it to the forefront of his mind, like now when he was sitting quietly, watching and remembering.

Cord knew his memories had driven him, but he also knew that Tabby's more recent encounter had given her the same motivation, and she too, was thinking about vengeance, although she had been instrumental in the exacting of some measure of vengeance, she was not satisfied, nor was Cord.

As he watched, he spotted two different groups of riders coming into town, both from the south side and the upper reaches of the valley of the Snake River, which also held the most active gold claims. But he had heard no gunfire, nor seen anything that could be considered outlawry, but he focused on the riders, and although he did not recognize all of them, each group had at least one familiar figure. They were not together, riding about a quarter mile apart, paying no attention to others, but not in any hurry. He watched as the first group of three stopped at the livery and disappeared inside. The second group, four riders, rode on into town, pulling up before the Big Dig saloon and tying off their mounts before going inside.

As Cord watched, the three that had put their horses in the livery, walked together and went into the same saloon as the other bunch. In the first group, Cord thought he recognized Buck Smithers, one of the earlier recruits. And in the second group, he was certain the tall, skinny one was the one called Gooseneck, a man that had been with them in Blackhawk when they struck the claim of Tabby and her brothers, and killed both brothers.

———

NEWT MORRISON WAS WAITING for the return of his men, sitting at a table in the corner with Yaqui as they watched the door for the return of the others. Buck Smithers led his men into the bar, spotted Morrison and walked to the table to take a seat. Newt nodded to Buck, ignored the others and looked back to the door to see the three men enter, one being Gooseneck. The last three took chairs at the next table, and Newt stood to talk to them all.

"We've found their camp, an' we're gonna hit it, kill him, an' take her. Then we'll have our way 'round'chere without any interfering! After we finish with them, I'm takin' over as sheriff, then Buck here," nodding to Buck Smithers who sat across the table from him, "an' Yaqui an' Fred there,"—nodding to a new face who was seated with Gooseneck at the side table—"will be muh leaders. Buck an' Yaqui's been with me right along, and Fred there, wal, he was with us back in the war an' after. He come out here to jin' up with us after gittin' outa jail in Kansas." He looked around at the men as they mumbled among themselves, looking at one another, sizing up their new leaders and more.

"Now, for our takin' them two whut done in th' others, we're splittin' up into three bunches. Me'n

Buck an' Elmer will come from up the hill above 'em, an' Yaqui, you'n Gooseneck, Willy, Chapo an' Fred, you'll come from below. Yaqui, you'n Gooseneck from the north side. Fred, you'n Willy an' Chapo from the south side. Nobody does nothin' till we come from uphill. Got that?" he growled, looking from one to the other.

With nods from all around, Newt looked at Buck and Elmer, "Let's go!" He looked at Yaqui and Fred, "All the rest of you, give us about enough time for you'all to have one drink, then come on." They nodded back and watched as Newt and his two men left the Big Dig saloon. Yaqui motioned to the barkeep for drinks all around and the man hustled to get the drinks, bringing just the glasses and two bottles. But Yaqui poured the drinks, capped the bottles and led the men as they downed the drinks, then looked at the others, "If we do this, we'll have this valley wide open for whatever we want!" and chuckled as he finished his drink.

16

ASSAULT

CORD RECOGNIZED NEWT MORRISON AS HE AND BUCK Smithers and one other man came from the saloon, walking quickly toward the livery. He kept them in sight until they disappeared into the stables, then swung the binoculars back to the saloon. Nothing stirred except for a lazy dog lying on the boardwalk next to the saloon at the general store as he got up to find some more shade. When the dog paused, lifted his head, Cord looked back to the saloon and saw others coming out and grabbing the reins of the tethered horses at the hitchrail and walking toward the livery. They no sooner started on their way, and the swinging doors at the saloon were pushed wide and five more came out, all headed the same way.

Hmmm...somethin' must be up, now what would they all be doing and probably together? mulled Cord as he watched, but three of them, Newt, Buck, and one more, rode out of the livery just as the others made it to the stables. Cord frowned, watched Newt lead the two men south out of town, but when the road bent to the west, they left the road and took a trail to the east that would take them up the draw beside Cord's camp.

He swung the binoculars back to the livery in time to see the five others, now mounted, come from the livery and go north, but keeping to the east edge of the road. Cord had that prickly sensation climb up his back, and his gut stirred with apprehension. *Something's up, and I don't like it, they're coming our direction and it looks like an ambush.* He came to his feet, called out to Tabby, "Saddle up! We're gettin' outta here! They're coming after us!" He ran to the stack of gear and started gearing up the mule, and once the packs were secured, he swung the saddle on Kwitcher and stepped aboard just as Tabby did the same atop her sorrel mare, Cassi. She looked at him, "What's happening?"

"The whole bunch of 'em just left the saloon, mounted up, and some, led by Newt, are coming up that way," nodding to the south of their camp and the long gulch that fell from the crest of the higher mountains to drain runoff into the Snake River. "And the others are comin' around this way," pointing to the north side of their camp. "But they're further downhill, and I think we might get away if we take that trail where you stirred up that bear!" He looked down at Blue, "Go boy! Scout!" motioning to the trail. He glanced to Tabby, "You lead out, take the mule, and I'll watch the rear. Keep goin' no matter what!" he ordered, waving her to get moving.

The trail was heavy with pine needles and in places, deep with last season's aspen leaves. They moved quietly but quickly, usually at a quick step or trot and where the trail allowed, a canter. They cut across the face of the big shoulder of the mountain, staying undercover in the trees. Cord heard the two groups coming from below, but they were now behind them while Cord and Tabby continued around the point of the shoulder, the trail bearing to the east, still in the thick timber.

Cord slipped the Winchester from the scabbard, jacked a round into the chamber and lay the weapon across his pommel. He started to twist around in the saddle when he heard the breaking of branches and felt the sudden blow to his back as a bullet plowed a furrow across his shoulders. He slumped over the pommel, fought the pain and twisted to see where the shot came from. He heard shouts, "They're over here!" and saw movement. He brought Kwitcher to a stop, brought the rifle to bear and squeezed the trigger. He saw his target, a man wearing a black vest, be lifted off his saddle and crash into the brush at the foot of some pines. Cord dug heels to his stallion and Kwitcher responded, taking the trail in long strides. Another shot blasted and the whisper of the bullet and the cracking of limbs sounded close, but overhead. Cord slumped in his saddle, the pain in his back severe and he could feel the blood running down his back. He took a deep breath and leaned down on the horse's neck, "You gotta do it boy, I'm countin' on you!"

Cord could hear Tabby and the mule still moving on the trail, and he drove his feet deep in the stirrups. He heard horses coming from behind, now on the same trail, and he gritted his teeth, dug deep in his resolve and saw some trees ahead that might suit his purpose. He reined the big stallion into the bigger trees, slid to the ground with rifle in hand and took a position on one knee, next to a big ponderosa. He checked his rifle, saw the cartridge in the chamber, and steadied himself against the tree. The muted thuds of horse hooves came nearer, and as the trail bent and the rider came into view, Cord squeezed off his shot, immediately jacking another round in the chamber. Cord saw the first rider fall from his shot, recognized him as Yaqui, saw his forehead smashed and the back of his head gone. But another rider, who was new, jerked on his reins, trying to stop his horse, but Cord shot him at the base of his neck, shattering his upper chest and knocking him to the ground. Two horses now milled around on the trail, giving Cord time to get mounted and get clear.

Tabby had slowed, looking back for Cord and as he neared, "You alright?" she pleaded, frowning as she saw him hunkered over.

"Took a slug in the back, don't know how bad." He lifted up, looked at her, "Keep going!" he growled, and nudged Kwitcher to bump into the rump of the long-legged sorrel. Tabby shook her head, turned back to the trail, slapped legs to the sorrel and took off at a trot, kicked her into a canter, pulling the lead to the mule taut as she looked back to be certain that Cord was close behind. Satisfied, she focused her attention on the trail as it crested the shoulder of a long, broad ridge, kept moving through the timber until she saw the part in the trees as they neared the long avalanche trough, cleared of all timber, and quickly moved across, to drop off into cover in the trees and both take up a position to await the outlaws. Cord winced as he moved, but he was not about to let Tabby take the brunt of the charge.

The riders were close behind, but when the leader tried to rein up, the others crowded him on the narrow trail, pushing his mount into the clearing. Cord held fire, wanting to see how many were there, but when they started to dismount, Tabby squeezed off her first shot that took the big one in the lead. Cord thought it was Willy, but he was taking aim at the second man he had recognized as Chapo, and dropped the hammer on him to see the bullet drive him to the ground, his chest awash with blood. Only one other man showed and he tried to rein his mount around, but Tabby squeezed off her second shot, and the man fell from the saddle.

The smoke from the shooting drifted away, the horses stopped their milling about and found some grass at the tree line and dropped their noses into the greenery. Three bodies were crumpled at the edge of the trees, none moving. Cord glanced to Tabby, back to the bodies, and spoke softly, "We'll wait a little, just in case any of the others come lookin' for 'em."

Tabby nodded, turned her attention back to the mouth of the trail, her rifle still in position, a round in the chamber, and the hammer cocked. They waited in silence, until Tabby said, "Well, if we're gonna just sit here, strip off your duster and let me have a look at your wound."

Cord chuckled, looked to the trail, and started shedding his duster. He winced at the pain as he moved about, felt the flow of fresh blood down his back and heard and felt Tabby rip the back of his shirt open to get at the wound. "Fore you get too far, take another look up yonder, there's still a couple others we ain't seen yet, one of 'em bein' that big Newt Morrison. He's the one that I want more'n any o' the others."

Tabby did as suggested, climbed over the brush to have a better look at the trail and up and down the avalanche trough. She turned back to Cord, "Nothin' movin' anywhere. We gonna do anything about the dead ones over yonder?"

"Dunno yet. Finish this, an' maybe we'll get another campsite, get some rest, then decide."

"Wait... there's one missin'!" declared Tabby, shading her eyes with her hand as she peered across the avalanche path. Two horses stood, restlessly moving about, and two bodies were evident, but she knew she had dropped the third man, but frowned as she remembered she saw him drop from the saddle but did not see where the bullet struck. She looked back at Cord, "The last one, I hit him, saw him fall, thought that was it, but now there's only two horses and two bodies. He must not have been hit too bad." She stared at the others, looking around for the third man, but knew he had slipped away.

"Then we need to get gone from here. If he gets to the others and tells 'em where we are, they'll be coming after us." Cord struggled to stand, started toward the ground, tied Kwitcher, looked back to see Tabby drive her foot in the stirrup and swing up on the big sorrel. "You take the lead, but I think we'd do better if we dropped into the bottom," offered Cord, pointing to the valley at the base of the mountain they were on, "that's Peru Creek down there, an' if we go a little more west, I think there's a gulch, some call Chihuahua Gulch, that has a little creek an' a trail that cuts between a couple talus slopes, but opens to a big green valley that'll prob'ly have some elk, and I think we'd both like some elk steak!"

17

CHIHUAHUA

"Where's the rest of 'em?" growled Newt when he saw Fred Wynkoop coming from the trail that split the trees. Newt and Buck had stayed behind at the campsite that had been used by Cord and Tabby, they were sitting on the log and rock near the firepit, but there was no fire, just two disgruntled outlaws. Fred nudged his mount closer, reached inside his jacket and pulled out a bloody hand, looked at Newt and Buck and slid to the ground, hanging on to the saddle to stay upright.

"Whatsamatta? You hit?" snarled Newt, glancing from Fred to Buck, slowly shaking his head. He looked at Buck, "We had eight men, and I thought he'd show 'em how to do things, but what happens? He's th' only one what comes back!" He looked back to Fred, "Alright, what happened?"

"I dunno how it started. When me'n them two I was with got up here, they was gone, an' 'bout that time I heard a rifle shot. Thought they'd found 'em and kilt 'em, but then there was more shots, so we took off after 'em. Found them other two dead in the trail, took off after 'em an' when that fat boy busted outta the timber, they dropped him sudden like, an' the Mex right after. I was behind 'em, but the horses all spooked, I was tryin' to get mine under control, an' took a slug in the shoulder, found m'self on the ground an' the horses tryin' to stomp my head in, but they done quit shootin'. So...I lay there, looked around sneaky like, saw they wasn't lookin' so..." he shrugged. He looked around, "Ain'tchu got no coffee? I sure could use some 'fore I bleed t'death!"

"Oh, shut up! Let's get outta here," grumbled Newt, rising to mount up and leave. "I was lookin' for that woman, thot we'd have her in hand 'bout now..." he mumbled as he swung aboard and jerked the head of his mount around to get to the trail.

―――――

NEWT LED the men into the Big Dig saloon, looked around and stopped still, frowning at an unusual sight sitting at the table in the corner. His first thought was whatever it was had to be as big as a mountain and black as a shadow at midnight. A deep growl that sounded like it came from the bowels of Hades and echoed through the empty saloon, said, "Howdy Newt!"

"Moses? Moses Young? Surely it ain't!" stammered Newt as his forehead wrinkled into a frown. He took one step forward, let a slow grin split his face and he stuck out his hand as he started chuckling, "Been a long time, Moses!"

"I heard tell you was gettin' bags o' gold without ever touchin' a shovel!" The big man laughed, as he extended his big hand across the table that seemed too small for him. The tabletop held a half-empty whiskey bottle, an empty shot glass, and some scattered playing cards.

"Tryin' but ain't had too much luck. Ran into a little problem lately," began Newt, pulling a chair out to join Moses at the table. "But now that you're here, maybe things'll change for the better!"

Moses dropped his eyes, chuckled a little and gathered up the cards. "I don't do things like that no more. Been doin' alright on muh own," he fanned the cards before him to emphasize his point. He lay the cards down, leaned on the table and asked, "This the same one that dealt you some trouble o'er to Blackhawk and after...?" His voice rolled like distant thunder and captured the attention of everyone around. Although there were few others, the barkeep stood still, watching, knowing what Morrison had done before and fearful of what he might do again. The barkeep knew Morrison had left earlier with seven men, and returned with two and a surly attitude.

Newt dropped his eyes, turned to motion to the barkeep to bring him a glass, and looked back to

Moses. "Been thinkin' 'bout leavin' here, ain't none o' these claims showin' much. They been talkin' 'bout silver, but that don't do us any good. Can't take the raw ore an' do nuthin' with it like we can gold. Heard tell some o' these what left here have gone o'er to Oro City where we was before. We done alright there, but..."

"But what?" rumbled Moses.

"Same trouble there, dunno for sure, but best I can tell, it's a deputy marshal outta Denver City..." Shrugged Newt, pouring himself a drink.

"Maybe it'd be better to put some distance 'tween you an' him. He the one you was after today?"

"Mmhmm, an' he's got a woman with him that I'd like to get to know a little better," snarled the big man, shaking his head before downing the whiskey.

"Mmmhmmm, I heard 'bout you an' your way with wimmen. Might wanna rethink that, when you mess with women, especially a good one, all the men around are gonna be against you. If you was smart, but from what I hear that don't apply to you, you'd find yourself some new territory away from this'n."

Newt frowned at the bigger man, scowling as he tried to sort out what had been said. He was not too sure whether Moses had been impudent or insulting or just giving friendly advice. But Newt remembered Moses and the way he had handled himself back in Kansas and Missouri during the war, and knew he did not want to try him now. He lowered the glass, slowly shook his head, glanced to Moses and back to see if Buck and Fred had returned. Buck had taken the wounded man to the doctor and promised to be right back.

As Newt started to turn back to Moses, the doors slapped open, and Buck stepped inside, looked around and spotting Newt, he approached the table, frowned at Moses and looked at Newt. "Doc said Fred'll be alright, after a spell. Said he lost a lotta blood, might be too weak to ride..." shrugged Buck, glancing fearfully at the mountain of a man that sat opposite Newt. "I was thinkin'..." began Buck, "might be time to find better territory. We ain't been doin' too good 'round'chere."

Newt shook his head, looking from Buck to Moses and back. "I ain't used to runnin' an' you ain't used to thinkin', so maybe we better re-consider."

"What'chu mean you ain't used to runnin'? We been runnin' ever since Oro City!"

Newt glared at Buck, glanced to a grinning Moses, and shook his head. "Well, I have been thinkin' 'bout Fairplay, just like the sound of it."

———

CORD LET Tabby take the lead, but he relieved her of the pack mule, and waved Blue to scout before them. Tabby picked her way through the thicker timber, close-growing spruce and fir, and dropped off the steeper slope into the bottom where Peru Creek wound its way through the berry bushes and more.

After crossing the creek, she found a trail that turned upstream, and Cord nodded as she glanced back for his reassurance. It was only about a mile before the steep-sided mountains on their left split to show a little feeder creek coming from the high country. But the little creek was too rocky and the valley bottom too narrow for the horses, so they rode a little further to find a trail that cut into the big draw, hugging the steep timbered hillside just above the talus slopes of moss rock.

The trail stayed above the slide rock, keeping to the low side of the tree line, and moving up the Chihuahua Gulch. It was just a short distance before the trail split two talus slopes, dropped down to cross the little creek and turned back upstream. It was a small basin where they cut across the creek, and a shoulder of hillside that shielded the upper basin, but Cord called out, "Whoa up!" and nudged his grulla alongside the sorrel. "Can you smell 'em?"

Tabby frowned, looked at Cord like he was losing his mind, then turned to look up the gulch. She turned back to Cord, "Smell what?"

"Elk? There's prob'ly a big herd just o'er that shoulder there." He grabbed his Spencer from the scabbard and swung to the ground, handing the reins of the grulla to Tabby, "Wait here," he suggested and started making his way to the grassy shoulder at the upper end of the little basin. As he neared the crest, he hunkered down, moved in a crouch, and slowly, peeked over the crest. He grinned, dropped to his knees and moved closer, went to his belly and crawled a little closer still. He stretched out, took aim at a young spike bull at the edge of the big herd, focused his telescopic sight, took a breath and slowly squeezed the trigger. The big Spencer bucked and roared, spat lead and smoke, and when the smoke cleared, Cord saw the pale rumps of the running herd as they took to a narrow trail that led them into the timber and out of sight, but they left behind the targeted bull, now down on the grass and still.

Cord rolled to his side, looked back at Tabby with a broad smile, "Supper!" he declared as he struggled to stand, wincing at the pain from his wound, and walked back to fetch his mount and lead the others to the downed elk. He chuckled, "Now the work begins," he declared, "but fresh elk steak is the best!"

18

CHANGE

It came in the night, quiet and cold, never so much as a whisper, but when they were chilled awake and looked about, everything was still and white. The morning sky was showing a hint of blue, and the clouds of snow had moved away, leaving behind an indescribable beauty and quiet. Tabby looked over at the bundle of Cord, smiled and whispered, "Isn't it beautiful?"

Cord nodded, grinning, and asked, "Why are you whispering?"

A low giggle escaped the smiling face, and the twinkle in her eyes flashed as she kicked off the covers and came to her feet. She wrapped her arms around herself and shivered. "Ooooo, it's cold!"

"What'd you expect, sunshine an' roses? It is the first of September and we're in the high country." Cord slowly came from his bedroll, wincing at the pain in his back, slipped on his duster and grabbed a blanket to cover his shoulders, tossing one to Tabby. "Cover up. I'll get a fire goin'."

Once the fire was going, Tabby shed her blanket and set about making some breakfast. Most of the elk hung in the big ponderosa at the edge of their camp, but they had cut out the back straps, and Tabby cut some strips to hang over the fire to broil while the biscuits browned in the Dutch oven. She fried a few pieces of bacon for the grease to make some gravy and watched Cord as he picked his way through the trees to the shoulder of the hill that overlooked their camp. She knew he would spend his time in prayer and reading, but would not take long. He still struggled with the wound on his back, although she had used some of their salve, which was a blend of Balm of Gilead and osha root to *doctor* the deep bullet gouge. She had stitched it together and it had begun to scab, but it still hindered his movement and would take some time before he was totally healed.

Cord scanned their valley and the Chihuahua Gulch for any sign of life. At the upper end of the big basin, the elk herd had bedded down in the edge of the timber, there was fresh sign of wolves, but no sighting of the animals that had probably been attracted by the smell of blood and guts from their kill the day before. When no other sign of life showed itself, Cord lowered the binoculars and picked up the Bible for his time with the Lord. He looked around at the beauty of the fresh snow that hung in the pine trees and humbled the bushes and grasses, lay as a quiet blanket on the stark flanks of the mountains, and made the blue sky appear as the cobalt blue was made brighter by the contrasting snow.

Cord still struggled with his craving for vengeance, every memory of his family and the many conflicts with the outlaws angered his spirit and tensed every muscle, and he searched the scriptures time and again. He turned to a dog-eared page at Psalm 58:10 *The righteous shall rejoice when he seeth the vengeance: he shall wash his feet in the blood of the wicked...* But he also remembered and turned to Romans 12:19 *Dearly beloved, avenge not yourselves, but rather give place unto wrath: for it is written, Vengeance is mine; I will repay, saith the Lord.*

Cord lifted his eyes to heaven and asked, "So, what do I do? I can't just forget what was done to my family and to Tabby's brothers, can I?" He did not really expect to have a voice answer, but the turmoil still stirred his innards. He shook his head and rose to return to the camp.

"Mmm, smells good!" proclaimed Cord with a broad smile as he stood the Winchester against the nearby fir and took a seat on the big rock near the cookfire. Tabby smiled, handed him a full cup of fresh steaming coffee, which he gladly accepted. She sat back on another rock, glanced at the breakfast makings and lifted her own cup to her mouth. "So, did you and the Lord have a good talk or was it an argument?" She grinned as she sipped on the coffee, understanding the struggle Cord had, which was much the same as her own.

"Dunno. First I think we need to keep at it till they're all dealt with, whether it's to put 'em under or to put 'em behind bars or hang 'em high somewhere, then..." he shrugged as he continued, "Next time I think we oughta just leave 'em to the Lord and let *Him* deal with 'em." He shook his head as he lapsed into a bit of a daze filled with memories and promises.

"Well, I ain't ready to give up, but..." she lifted her eyes to Cord, saw the internal struggle in his eyes, and shook her head, "maybe if we just, well, I dunno, maybe leave this place and try to find some kinda peace somewhere else. But then there would always be that nagging in the back of my mind about getting vengeance or justice or somethin'."

"Ummhmmm," nodded Cord, showing his understanding.

"But...right now, how 'bout breakfast?"

Cord grinned, nodded and sat his cup down, picked up a tin plate and held it out for her to fill it up. They ate in silence, savoring the meal and the environment, but with troubled spirits as their memories would not let them rest, always bringing back images of the murdered loved ones.

———

"I FOUND 'EM!" cackled Fred Wynkoop as he stomped into the warm interior of the saloon. Snow fell from his boots and he doffed his hat to shake off the white stuff as he grinned at the three men at the table. Moses, Newt, and Buck glared at the talker. Newt growled, "What'chu mean, you found 'em?"

"Those two you were wantin', you know, the woman and the fella with her!"

"Where?" growled Newt, giving Fred his full attention, while Moses leaned back and glanced to Buck.

"Wal, I went back the way we did when they run from their camp. Followed the trail, cuz couldn't see no tracks in this snow. Went to where they kilt them others, by the avalanche chute, an' stepped down, looked around, and then I saw it! A thin trail of smoke comin' from acrost the creek, up a narrow draw 'tween the mountains. Has to be them, ain't nobody else would be there an' cookin' in this weather. Miners all got 'em cabins or been stayin' in town, so I'se sure it's them!"

"I ain't gonna be sure 'till we see 'em, but I ain't goin' out in this snow!" growled Newt, and glared at Fred. "You go back, get closer, an' when you see 'em and know it's them, you come back an' then we'll take 'em!" Newt shook his finger at Fred, "An' don' you go losin' 'em this time, y'hear?"

"Yeah, yeah, but I'm gonna get me some food an' hot coffee first. It's too cold out there! Gotta get warm first, then I'll go!" whined Fred, shaking his head and turning away from the three men. He stomped to the front door, now closed against the weather, and pushed outside to go to the *Summit Chop House* for some food. He grumbled as a cold blast of air whistled around his neck prompting him to turn up his collar and lower his head, quicken his step, driven by his hunger and the cold.

He limped toward the restaurant, favoring his bruised hip that reminded him of his close call the last time he pursued that woman and the fella with her. One of them had shot at him, the bullet ricocheting off the pommel of his saddle, striking his holstered pistol, and slamming it against his bony hip, knocking him to the ground. But he considered that his lucky shot, since the other two men had been killed. When the shooters thought he was dead, and turned to themselves, it gave him the chance to get away. Although the ricochet had cut his side, leaving some blood on the ground, it was only enough to make it sore, but it also gave him a constant reminder of his need for revenge.

"What'chu need, friend?" Cooky asked as he came to the table where Fred had tenderly lowered himself.

"Food! Anything you got, and lotsa coffee!"

Cooky nodded, frowning as he turned away to go to the kitchen and prepare a plate of food for the man. When he returned with some steak, potatoes, beans, and bread on the plate in one hand and a big cup of steaming coffee in the other, Fred grinned wide-eyed as he watched the man set the food before him. Cooky asked, "You been out in this weather this mornin'?"

"Ummhmm, lookin' for them two that shot muh pards. Almost had 'em yestiddy, but..." he shrugged as he reached for the coffee. He took a big sip, added, "But I foun' 'em and we'll get 'em!" nodding his head as he agreed with himself.

Cooky frowned, "So, who's these two you huntin'?"

"Ah, just some woman and a fella with her. Newt's the one what wants the woman. He's like that!"

"An' where'd you find 'em?" asked Cooky, trying his best to be nonchalant as he flipped a rag over his shoulder, put his free hand on his hip as he poured another cup of coffee for the man. He had left the pot there on his first trip, poured the cup full to return to the kitchen, wanting to know where this man had been.

"Don't matter where they is, we're gonna get 'em. I gots to go make sure it's them, and come back an' tell Newt. Then we'll go!" he grumbled, more interested in his food than anything else at this point.

Cooky nodded, and with coffeepot in hand, returned to the kitchen. He thought about Cord and Tabby, almost certain these were the two this man and the others were after. Had to be since they were the ones that fit the description. There was not another woman in this entire valley that would be riding in the mountains with a man. There were only three other women in the town and none of them would be riding a horse anywhere. He chuckled as he thought of the woman known as gran'ma by everyone. She was the white-haired tough woman who had her own claim and was meaner than most of the other sourdoughs in the valley. The other two women were not the type to go outside much, nor ride a horse anywhere, as they plied their trade after dark.

He set the coffeepot down, furrowed his brow as he sat on the tabletop and thought. Maybe...maybe I could follow him, or...maybe I could just backtrack him and warn Cord. I think... He chuckled, slipped off the table and went to his closet to get some warmer clothes for his journey. Cooky was looking forward to getting out of the restaurant for a while and getting some fresh mountain air that smelled like something beside dirty miners, burnt steaks, and reheated potatoes.

19

WARNING

THE EARLY AFTERNOON SUN WAS DOING ITS BEST TO MAKE the first snowfall retreat, leaving behind only the blown drifts that lay in the shadows. The trail that led from the earlier campsite of Cord and Tabby, rode the shoulder of the timbered hillside to bend back to the east to follow Peru Creek into the high-country valley. Cooky found it easy to follow the muddy tracks of Fred Wynkoop as he sought to return to where he believed Cord and Tabby were camped. Cooky kept watch on the trail before him, stopping to listen often, needing to ensure he left the trail before Wynkoop returned. Cooky watched from the trees when Fred dropped off the timbered hillside into the valley bottom to cross Peru Creek and continue upstream. Cooky stepped down, shading his eyes to watch from the edge of the avalanche path, to see where the outlaw left the trail. When he saw Wynkoop turn onto a narrow trail that headed up

Chihuahua Gulch, Cooky remounted and nudged his horse through the trees to follow.

———

CORD BELIEVED they were safe and their campsite unknown, but he was bothered by that nagging, crawling up his spine, sensation that usually forebode something wrong. With a glance to Tabby, he grabbed up his Spencer, the binoculars, and said, "I'm goin' to take a look at our backtrail. It's probably nothin' but..." he shrugged. Their camp was nestled within the trees behind a slight rise that held thick black timber, and where the trail into the basin bent around the lower basin that was thick with bogs, standing water, and beaver dams, before turning toward their camp. It was on that rise with the black timber that Cord had made his promontory and place of prayer. It was only from there that he could see across the lower bog, and to the lower reaches of the Chihuahua Gulch that held the only trail with access to their camp.

As he approached the little clearing, Cord went to one knee and lifted the binoculars, scanning the gulch, the bog bottom, and the trail below. Nothing moved. He took a more comfortable position, sitting with his knees raised and slowly scanned the entire bottom and lower trail. At first, nothing moved, but he moved the binoculars back to the lower trail and there, came a lone rider, obviously searching the hills around as he slowly came up the trail. He stopped, slipped to the ground and led his mount into the trees, soon returning, carrying a rifle held across his chest as he looked around, obviously searching for something or someone and a little nervous as he carefully picked his way along the tree line, moving up the trail.

Cord lowered the binoculars, picked up his Spencer with the long telescopic sight, and lifted it to watch the intruder to their domain. As the man moved, he often looked to the trail for any sign, but with the snowfall and melting snow, there would be no distinguishable tracks, but still, he came. Cord noticed that the man often looked in the direction of the rise where he sat, shaded his eyes and searched the valley as best he could without field glasses or telescope. Cord frowned as he watched, keeping the man in view with his telescopic sights, always ready to drop the hammer on him if necessary.

But the man stopped when the trail turned back to the east and pointed toward their camp. The trail had hugged the lower flank of the west mountains, staying just below the tree line, but as the contour of the land changed, the trail turned east to cross the bottom of the basin below another high-country pond and nearby bog, water that would freeze solid in mid-winter but now provided flow to the little creek that came from the upper end of the gulch. It was in the black timber on the lower east side of this basin where Cord and Tabby made their camp. Cord watched as the man moved back into the trees, hiding behind the thicker woods. Cord glanced toward their camp, nothing showed, no smoke rose, nothing to give away their presence. He frowned, wondering if this was what this man was looking for —their camp.

Cord knew he could send the intruder scampering by throwing a round into the trees where he thought himself to be hidden, and it would be easy with his Spencer and the telescopic sight, but he knew that would also be a positive giveaway about their presence. He decided to wait for the skulking sneak to make the first move, and he waited.

He sensed movement from behind, and Cord twisted around to see Tabby leading the two horses and mule from the trees. She was headed to the pond to water the animals and let them have some graze, something he would usually do, but he was on lookout duty. He looked back to the trees that held the intruder. Again, there was no movement, but Cord continued his vigil. After the animals had their drink, Tabby picketed the three to graze and casually walked back toward their camp, looking for edibles as she strolled. Cord grinned, shook his head and chuckled to himself, knowing she had no way of knowing that two men and only one being friendly were watching her every move. But she soon disappeared back into the trees, unharmed.

Cord turned his attention back to the man in the trees, and within moments, he emerged, carefully taking to the edge of the trees to return to where he left his tethered horse. Cord lowered the Spencer, lifted the more powerful binoculars and watched as the man rode from the narrow gulch, staying to the trail, often looking over his shoulder to see if he was followed. When he disappeared into the Peru Creek valley, Cord went back to their camp. He believed the man had accomplished just what he wanted—to find their camp.

Blue jumped up to welcome Cord back to the camp and Cord bent to rub the dog behind his ears and talk to him as they walked together back into the camp to be greeted by a smiling Tabby. "How's your back?" she asked as she cut the thick elk rump meat into long thin strips to be smoked.

"Sore, but gettin' better," he answered, wincing as he moved, twisting his trunk around and feeling the bandages and scabbing at the long wound. "But don't go smokin' that meat quite yet," he said, nodding to her work.

"Why not? We need to get it smoked 'fore we leave, don't we?"

"Yeah, but we've had comp'ny. A lone rider came up the gulch, tethered his mount in the trees and came further on foot. He was hiding in the trees when you came out with the horses. I think he was just trying to locate our camp for the others, and he didn't see it till you came out."

"Oh," she replied, frowning and turning to look at Cord, fearful of what he was thinking.

"I'm guessin' he was probably with the rest of the Red Legs and went back to report our whereabouts, so we might be needin' to move 'fore they come back."

"I was just getting to like this place, kinda thinkin' about it as home," she drawled, looking around their cozy camp.

The sudden hail that came from beyond the trees startled both of them, "Hello, the camp!" and Cord, with the Spencer still in hand, moved quickly to the edge of the trees to see who was approaching. He spotted a man riding a dark blood bay, stopped on the trail below the rise and beyond the camp. He looked a little familiar and Cord thought of Cooky, but he had never seen the man without his apron and he was not too sure. But Cord answered, "Come on in if you're friendly!"

Cord recognized Cooky as he came near. "Well, I sure did not expect to see you up here! Where's your apron?"

"Ain't cookin' today—had to come warn you. There was a man with the bunch of outlaws who came in today tellin' the big guy, Newt, that he found your camp. But Newt, when he found out all he saw was smoke, sent him back to make sure it was your camp. I followed him, saw him come up here and then leave, I was in the trees on the other side, and he was in a hurry. I wanted you to know they's prob'ly gonna come up here after you!" declared Cooky.

"I saw him and thought that might be what he was doin' comin' up this way. When he left, he had seen our horses down in the bottom yonder, so, he knows we're here."

"What'chu gonna do?" asked Cooky as he stepped down, twisting side to side and stretching. He mumbled, "Ain't been on a horse in some time, muh muscles ain't used to it!"

Cord looked at Tabby, back to Cooky. "Reckon we oughta just leave, but I'd kinda like to get it over an' done with here'n now." He looked back to Tabby who nodded her agreement.

"I'm all for that," suggested Tabby, "even if we left, it'd still be hangin' o'er our heads and ever' time we thought about it, we'd wish we'd stayed, so..." she shrugged, looking to their packs and going to fetch her rifle.

"Well, Cooky, thanks for the warning. I think we need to get busy and see if we can set things up to our advantage," stated Cord, reaching out his arm for Tabby to come near.

Cooky looked from one to the other, "Well, good luck. I'll have somethin' special waitin' for your supper if'n you wanna come into town after..." he drawled as he swung back aboard the big bay. With a wave, he reined his mount around and started back on the trail.

Cord called after him, "Make sure they don't meet you on the trail!"

Cooky waved again and was soon out of sight. Cord looked at Tabby, "Any ideas?"

"That's your job, not mine!" letting a nervous laugh spill out.

Cord looked up at the sun, around at the camp, and sat down, thinking as he looked about. He looked at Tabby, "How 'bout some coffee?"

"You gonna think better with coffee?" she asked.

"Mebbe..." he drawled, smiling. "What I'm thinkin' is, it's getting late. By the time that rider gets back to town, gives his story, and the others get mounted to come out here, it'll be gettin' dark, and the way they work, they'd probably prefer to hit us in the dark, shoot us in the bedrolls while we're sleepin'."

"Sounds 'bout right..."

"So, here's what I'm thinkin'..." began Cord, watching Tabby stir up the coals and push the coffee pot closer to the flames.

20

RAID

THE SETTING SUN WAS CRADLED IN THE CUT BETWEEN THE towering peaks on the west side of the valley. Ruby Gulch split the granite tips, giving a path for runoff to cut through the lower timber. All the mountains that surrounded the basin of the Chihuahua Gulch, rose high above timberline and stood naked in the golden light of the last moments of the day. On either side of the gulch, black timber lay quiet as short skirts on the flanks of the mountains, a thin tendril of smoke lifting slowly above the black timber to be colored by the sunset. The camp of Cord and Tabby lay still, the low embers of supper's fire gasping the last smoke, and the dim light that filtered through the tall trees showed the still forms of two wrapped comfortably in warm blankets, saddles for pillows. The only other living thing was the restless mule, tethered well back into the trees, agitated hooves shuffling in the pine needles, head tossing in the loose tethered halter.

Hooves rattled on the shale and moss rock of the talus slope that fell below the trees at the mouth of the gulch. Cord was on his promontory on the shoulder of timber below their camp, watching the trail below and was alerted when he heard the shod hooves of horses coming up the draw. He knew sound carries easily in the late hours of day and early hours of night, he had counted on hearing the approach of whoever would dare come to their camp. He also believed that anyone coming at this hour had evil intent and he held no qualms about what was to come. He turned toward their camp, gave a low whistle with three notes, to tell Tabby there were three riders coming.

When the incoming riders followed the trail, it took them across the base of the talus slope, crossed the creek in the bottom and followed the tree line over the saddle of the ridge, before opening into the lower basin. The trees on the west slope ended at the grassy edge of the basin that held the bogs, beaver dams, and stagnant ponds. The trail stayed at the tree line, continuing north up the long valley, until the slight rise between the lower basin and the second basin that carried the trail east to the edge of the trees below Ruby Gulch and the site of Cord and Tabby's camp.

Cord's promontory gave him an unhindered view of the trail and he watched the three riders as they pushed their horses into the trees and dismounted. The full moon hung high over the eastern line of peaks, almost daring the setting sun to linger but watched the brighter orb slip below the horizon. The light of dusk still allowed Cord to see the three men, now on foot, take to the trail out of necessity to avoid the ponds and bogs, and cross the little creek. Cord saw the bigger man motion and point, making the two others spread out as they began their slow and stealthy approach.

Cord had already chosen his firing point, the ragged stump of a winter kill pine, the irregular shape offering him all the cover he needed. He had already calculated the distance, taking into account he was shooting downhill. It was just over a hundred yards, and he could easily see each of the men. His first target would be the big man in the middle, who he thought was Newt Morrison, and without their leader, the others would be less of a threat but still targets. Cord also had chosen a secondary firing point, closer to their camp and lower down the hill, but still well protected in the trees.

Tabby had taken a spot on the north side of the trail, further up from the turn-off to the camp, and well protected in the trees. She stood behind the big trunk of a tall ponderosa that stretched tall among the fir, but near a towering spruce. She had a good field of fire, the trail exposed to her view and the dim light of dusk. If she took a shot before they neared the tree line, they would be easily seen, but once in the shadows of the trees, it would be difficult.

From the crossing of the creek to the tree line and the turn-off to their camp, was about two hundred yards. A good distance for the approaching men to be in the open and the fading light. Cord waited until they were facing into the remaining light of dusk and the colors of the sunset, lifted his Winchester and took aim at the chest and side of the big man, took a good breath and let some out and began a slow squeeze of the trigger, all the while following the slow-moving figure.

The rifle bucked, driving back against Cord's shoulder, spitting flame that lit up the approaching darkness, and sent its messenger of death on its way. Cord jacked another round into the chamber, saw the first round strike the big man, causing him to stumble but not go down, and Cord took aim on the man again. He squeezed off another shot before the echoing of the first died, and the rifle spat fire, smoke and lead again, taking the target as he fought to gain his feet, but drove him down onto his face.

Cord had no sooner fired the first round than he heard the blast from the far side of the trail and saw flame stab from the shadows, and the man on the far side of Morrison, who had turned toward Cord, searching for the shooter, took the bullet in the back of his neck, splattering blood on the dying form of Newt Morrison. Cord moved his rifle to take aim on the third man, who started to scramble to the trees, but Cord followed the fleeing figure, squeezed off his shot at the same time that the rifle from the shadows belched fire and lead, and the third man stumbled, fell face first into the dirt, and did not move again.

Cord jacked another round, looked at each of the men, saw no movement, waited a few moments, and there was still no movement, then rose and started from the trees. He approached the nearest downed form, saw the black shadow of blood on his back, but no sound nor move. He nudged the body with the toe of his boot, and was satisfied the man was dead. He saw Tabby coming from the trees, watched her as she neared, glancing often to the other two downed outlaws, and waited until she came alongside. She was breathing heavy, and looked at Cord, "Is it over?"

"Maybe, need to check the other two, but I think so," he answered, as he looked toward the other two and started that direction. Tabby walked beside him, both keeping their rifles at the ready, and they looked at the big man, and Cord paused, lifting his rifle as he frowned, watching the figure on the ground. Tabby kept walking until Cord said, "Wait..." but the big man lifted a pistol toward Tabby, but she dropped to one knee and lifted her rifle and fired.

The bullet from the rifle took the man in his big chest, driving him back, but he fired his pistol, the bullet going wild. Tabby came to her feet, jacking another round in the chamber as she stepped closer, the muzzle of the rifle pointing at the big man. Newt Morrison groaned, struggling for breath and tried to lift his pistol, but Tabby's Winchester roared, again and again, as with each step she jacked a round, fired, and repeated, driving at least six more bullets into the body of Morrison. With each blast, the big man's body jerked, blood splattered, spittle flew, and angry eyes flared, but each lead slug drove life further and further from the man's grasp, and when she stood over him, she glared at the bloody pulp and spat on his face.

Cord stepped beside her, reaching his arm around her shoulders and pulled her close. She buried her face in his chest, sobbing, not for Morrison, but for the memory of her brothers who had given their lives to protect her and whose lives had been taken by this man and his outlaws. She turned around and looked at him again, spat on his bloody form, and turned back to stomp away to their camp.

Cord let her go, glanced to the third man and walked to his form, making certain he was dead with a nudge from his boot. Satisfied, he started back to the trees, going to where they had picketed the horses further from the camp for their safety. The last thing he wanted was for either of the horses or their dog, Blue, who had been ordered to stay with the horses, to be wounded or killed by a stray bullet.

When he led them into their camp, Tabby had already stirred up the coals and had the coffeepot dancing. She sat on a rock near the flames, staring into the fire, remembering. Cord picketed the horses near the mule, walked to the fire, sat his rifle against the tree near their saddles, and sat down opposite Tabby. She glanced at him but said nothing, returning to her moment of recollection and reverie. When the coffee appeared to be ready, Cord pulled the pot back, poured a little cold water in the pot to settle the grounds, then poured two cups of coffee, handed one to Tabby, and with his cup cradled in both hands, sat back and sighed.

21

DECISIONS

"So, now what?" asked a resolute Tabby as she worked at finishing packing the panniers and packs.

"Well, we'll take the bodies and gear into town, maybe talk to Cooky and any others that might be interested, and see if they'd be willing to get themselves a sheriff or..." shrugged Cord as he tightened the latigo. He stepped back, looked at Tabby. "While you finish here, I'm goin' to get their horses and bring them back to the bodies and start loading. Then we can go into town."

Tabby gave a weak grin, turned away to finish her work and as Cord rode from their camp, she turned to watch. Her thoughts were running askew, confusion and concern blending with a measure of relief. She had wanted the murderers of her brothers caught and punished, but what she had pictured was jail and a trial and then... her anger had boiled over last night with the attack by the outlaws, apparently bent on doing what they often did—raid, murder, steal and anything else that suited them. She knew the leader, Newt Morrison, had been wanting to get her and make her his own woman. That had been said when they had captured and used her as bait before, but she had escaped, thanks to Cord. But now she was alone, facing an uncertain future with limited resources and no particular direction. She glanced to the trees where Cord had disappeared, thought of him and their growing friendship. She had begun thinking of him as more than just a friend and protector, but she was uncertain of what he thought. She believed it was his nature to protect the weaker, but it seemed like more than that, but was it just wishful thinking? She took a deep breath that lifted her shoulders, stood up with hands on hips and looked around to be certain she was not forgetting anything, and began to load the panniers, packs and parfleches onto the packsaddle of the mule.

Although the sun was full up, it still hid itself behind the tall mountains that surrounded the narrow Chihuahua Gulch until the trail took them to the bottom of the valley that carried Peru Creek. They turned to the west, leaving the rising sun to warm their backs until the trail crossed Peru Creek and turned south alongside the Snake River. It was just over a mile from the Peru Creek to the north end of Montezuma. Cord led the way, leading the three loaded horses, followed by Tabby, leading the pack mule. They had no sooner entered the town and the few people on the street gawked at the unusual sight of horses loaded with dead bodies. The word spread faster than the horses moved, and people gathered on the boardwalk, some stepping into the street to get a closer look and maybe identify the bodies.

One man walked beside the first horse, lifted the head of the dead man by his hair and quickly loosed his grip, turned to the people on the boardwalk. "It's Newt Morrison and some o' his men!" he shouted. More people came from the Summit Chop House, including Cooky who stepped out, wiping his hands on a small towel and frowning at the sight before him. He nodded to Cord, looked at the others, and along with several of the men, followed the string to the livery. At the front door of the livery, Cord reined up, stepped down and called out to the smithy, "Hey Smithy!"

The grizzled smithy stepped into the big doorway and asked, "What'chu want?"

"You had a helper the other day, I think you called him Moose, he around?"

"What'chu wan' him fer?"

"Got a job for him. I need him to dig three graves an' put these men under. I'll pay him a dollar a grave!"

From the side of the door stepped a gangly young man who stood at least six feet tall, broad chest and shoulders, high water britches held up by galluses, bare feet and a raggedy shirt. His dirty blonde hair hung in his face and he never seemed to shut his mouth, his lower lip always drooping. He stepped into the light, "How much?"

"A dollar a grave, and there's three that need buryin'."

"I'll do it!" he answered, walking to the horses and grabbing the lead of the first. He looked up at Cord, "When do I get paid?"

"I'll pay you when you bring the horses back here," answered Cord. "Now, bury 'em deep."

"I done it 'fore, I know how to dig 'em," drawled the young man, looking over his shoulder at Cord as he led the horses toward boot hill.

Cord looked at the smithy, "You wanna buy those horses and saddles?"

"How much?"

"Fifty dollars for everything."

"Done!" declared the smithy.

"We'll be at the chop house," explained Cord, leading Kwitcher as he turned away, looked at the crowd, and pushed through. Tabby followed him the short distance to the Chop House where they tethered the animals and walked inside. Cooky was standing behind the counter, grinning as they entered, "Glad to see you made it alright. When'd they come?"

"'Bout an hour or so after you left. Gave us time to get set for 'em," explained Cord, taking a seat at a table with Tabby.

Cooky brought cups and coffee, poured the cups

full, one for himself as well, and sat down. "Now what?"

Cord lifted his cup, took a long drink, sat it down and leaned on the table, looking at Cooky. "You think any of these townspeople are willing to step up and become sheriff, or at least support a sheriff?"

Cooky dropped his eyes, slowly shook his head and looked back up at Cord, "Don't think so. Most of 'em are too busy with their own needs, prospectin', minin', what-have-you. They might support a sheriff, but won't be one."

"What about the other businesses? Think they might?"

"Maybe, but what do you have in mind?"

"Well, with the worst of the bunch done in, I thought they'd at least want somebody around so it won't be so tempting for the next wannabe bad man to try doin' the same thing these others were doin', you know, hittin' the prospectors and such like they did to Zabrisky and others."

Cooky frowned, replied, "I know we need it, but I don't know who, what about you?"

Cord shook his head. "Can't. We'll be leavin' soon. But I'll talk to 'em if you can get 'em together."

Cooky nodded, then his grin turned into a frown. "You also need to know that might not be all of 'em. There's a big colored man, makes out to be a gambler, but the smithy said he was talkin' with Newt like they were old pals. Then two other men came in, joined 'em, and they spent the rest of the night in the Big Dig saloon, talkin' and playin' cards. But Newt and his two left, and the big man and two new ones stayed back. One of those new men dresses like a dandy, fancies himself a gambler also, he carries a pistol in a shoulder holster, but I've not seen a weapon on the big man, prob'ly don't need one. The other'n, well, compared to the others, he looked purty scruffy, but he was cocky, always kept his hand on his pistol, had shifty eyes." He paused, shook his head and continued, "I don't know where they been stayin', in the hotel or camped out or..." he shrugged. "You might wanna be careful, you know," he added.

"Well, how 'bout fixin' us somethin' to eat?" asked Cord. He glanced to Tabby who was smiling at the suggestion of having a meal she did not have to cook.

Cooky was glad to return to the safe haven of his kitchen and puttered around for a short while and soon returned with plates full of food. As he set the plates down, the door swung open and the men he just spoke of, walked in together, looking around, and when they spotted Cord and Tabby, it was obvious who they were searching for, but they sat down, looked at Cooky and waved him over to their table.

After Cooky took their order, they huddled together, talking to one another a bit louder than necessary, but with their continual leering looks toward Tabby, their banter was more lewd and suggestive than what was normally acceptable in public places. Several of the other diners hurriedly finished their meal and left, but the leering looks and remarks continued, even after their food was delivered.

Cord and Tabby finished their meal, rose to leave, but to exit the front door, they had to walk past the table of the three men. As they neared, the scruffy one leaned back in his chair as if to block their path. Tabby was ahead of Cord and did not slow her pace, but as she neared the man, he reached toward her, only to have her quickly draw her Colt pocket pistol, slam it down on the man's wrist with the barrel and bring the Colt to full cock and stick the muzzle in the man's ear.

"You need to mind your manners!" she growled, shoving the pistol hard against his head, making him drop his chair to the floor and try to grab at the pistol, but she quickly drew back and slammed it down on the top of his head, knocking him unconscious and face first to the table, splattering his meal with his face.

The two other men stared wide-eyed at Tabby, looked to Cord, who was grinning as he watched. With his hand resting on the butt of his pistol under the duster, Cord looked at the other men and said, "She doesn't tolerate bad manners."

They nodded to the others and walked out while the two gamblers stared at their backs. When Cord started to open the door, the big Black man spoke with his deeper than thunder voice, "Those men you brought in were my friends."

"Those men were cowardly back-shooting sneak thieves and deserved everything they got. And if these,"—motioning with a wave of his hand to the other two men at the table—"are the same type, I suggest you work on choosing better friends."

22

___

BRAWL

The rude trio of gamblers and bad men followed Cord and Tabby outside, with the unconscious character held up by the other two. Cord and Tabby had started toward the hotel on the same side of the street and were on the boardwalk when the big man hollered, "I'm gonna tear you apart and stomp on your remains! Those were my friends you killed and I'm gonna make you wish you'd never seen 'em!" The big man's deep thunderous voice rolled across the street, filling the town with his growling roar. He dropped his burden, started stomping toward Cord, each step rattling the boardwalk and seeming to roll across the town like an earthquake. Cord turned to look, shook his head and spoke softly to Tabby, "Stay back, this is gonna get ugly!" and began shedding his duster and pistol belt.

He glanced toward the big man, dropped his duster and pistol belt over the hitchrail and walked into the street. With every step, memories of his youth and his father flooded back. His father had fought with the British and the Ottoman Empire during the revolt of Tripolitania. It was during that time he learned from some men of Thailand the skills of Muay Thai fighting. During all of Cord's youth, his father taught him the skills he knew in this type of fighting and more, and at every outing, he tested Cord, teaching him more moves and ways of countering any attack. His training lasted from before his teens, until his family was murdered before Cord turned eighteen. His father often said, *"When you don't have the size, you must have the skills. This type of fighting will give you the confidence and skill you need to defend yourself and others. Always remember, a man with confidence and skill and with right on his side, will be undefeatable."*

As Cord moved into the middle of the street, there was nothing about him that would appear imposing to anyone, but he showed no fear, no threat of fleeing, just a relaxed confidence. But when compared to the mountain of a man known as Moses, none of the watchers thought this would be much of a fight.

Moses had also stripped off his jacket, pushed up his sleeves and with his head slightly lowered, he used his deep voice to roll thunderous threats across the street, glaring with contempt at Cord as he approached. "You are gonna be like that mud puddle yonder, nothin' left of you but your blood and guts to soak into the ground!"

Cord stood still, watching the way the big man moved, massive arms to his side, ham hock fists clenched before him, muscles bulging under the linen shirt, his arms, chest, and shoulders rippling in the midday sun. Judging the man's moves as he had been taught, looking for any weakness or overconfidence, things his father repeatedly taught him. The spectators were speechless, fearful for the lesser man, but none leaving nor turning away, all held by the threat and promise of a fight.

The men began to circle one another, Cord now with his hands lightly clenched and held easily before him, watching every move, noticing the movement of Moses's feet as he shifted his weight to his toes, his eyes, never wavering and focused on Cord's eyes, and the clenching and unclenching of his fists.

Cord flexed his body, moving his feet, shoulders, arms and more. He knew that most men knew what they thought to be boxing, or using their fists to deliver blows to their opponent. Some would also try wrestling their opponent to the ground and overpower them. But Muay Thai uses more than just fists, or strength, it uses the *'Art of 8 limbs'* or every part of their body. Cord was very agile and deceptively strong, and although usually confident, this man before him was one of the biggest men he had ever seen, more of a mountain than a man, and his strength was obvious.

Moses threw the first punch, a jab to Cord's face, but Cord moved just enough for the massive fist to pass by, making the big man stumble. He thought he would connect and knock Cord to the ground and threw all his weight behind the punch, but when he missed, his balance was thrown, and he stumbled, confusion showing on his face. Cord deftly stepped aside, untouched and making no move against Moses.

Moses growled, glared at Cord, roared and charged, expecting to wrap his arms around Cord, but when he grasped, there was nothing there. Cord had ducked away, twisting to the side, and stepped behind the big man, and chuckled.

Moses glared, thundered, "Why don'tchu stand and fight like a man!"

"Man? I thought I was watchin' a mountain or a mule or maybe a grizzly bear, but not a man!" responded Cord, stepping just out of reach of the big man.

Moses squinted his eyes, his nostrils flaring and his teeth clenched as he growled and started a roundhouse swing, but Cord spun around and away, bringing up his right foot and in the momentum of the spin, buried the heel of his foot in the big man's side. The blow knocked Moses off his balance and he stumbled but did not fall. He appeared shocked and looked back at Cord, confusion showing on his face.

Moses charged at Cord, both fists lifted and ready. He jabbed with his left, readied his right for a roundhouse. Cord ducked under the jab, did another spin, and as he turned, Moses had prepared another jab, and expecting another kick, stepped away, but Cord leaned in and smashed the back of his elbow against Moses's jaw, knocking the man off his feet, falling to the ground. But Moses caught himself and quickly regained his feet, shaking his head and looking around. He found Cord standing, waiting, and showing no fear.

Again, Moses glared, growling, but approached his quarry more wary and cautious. Cord slowly moved counterclockwise, almost in a dance, always watching the big man, and when Moses stepped forward, driving his massive fist toward Cord as he growled, Cord sidestepped him. He used his own and his opponent's momentum, and swept the big man's feet out from under him with a quick spin and using his own leg as the weapon.

But Moses jumped to his feet, frustrated, angry, but unhurt. Cord knew the big man had not been hurt, for all his moves had done nothing but drop him to the ground. Now, the man was mad and more dangerous than ever. He stomped toward Cord, growling and glaring, his teeth clenched and his eyes almost slits. He neared Cord, spread his arms wide, ready to grab Cord and crush him to death. Cord feinted one way, bent the other way, but the big man was wary and surprisingly agile and quick for such a big man. As Cord started to turn away, Moses grabbed his arm and jerked him back to his chest, wrapping his arms around him. As Moses began to squeeze, Cord felt his chest starting to crush and kicked his feet out, dropping all his weight against the big man. Moses let a roar come from deep in his chest, and he lifted Cord off the ground, tossed him into the air and grabbed him, lifting him overhead and throwing Cord like a piece of wood. Cord went spinning and tumbling through the air, trying to catch his wind, but crashed into a hitchrail, smashing it into kindling.

The impact robbed Cord of his wind, but he knew he had to move, although his whole body felt broken. He slowly rolled to one side, saw the bear of a man stomping his way, and Cord rolled away, slowly came to his feet, and gasping for breath, looked at the big man and forced a grin as he slowly shook his head.

Moses stomped closer, spreading his arms wide and growled, "That was just for fun, now I'm gonna crush the life outta you!"

But Cord seemed to sprout springs on his feet and jumped high, kicked the big man in his solar plexus, almost burying his moccasined foot in his chest, causing him to choke and start to bend over. Cord dropped to the ground, reached up and grabbed the back of the big man's head, jerked it toward the ground and met his face with his knee. The blow smashed the man's nose across his face, broke his front teeth and his jaw, dropping him to the ground, choking on his own blood and bile from the nerve center of his body that nestled behind his solar plexus.

Cord stepped back, watching the man struggle. The crowd had grown quiet, but a glance showed the two friends of Moses start to move toward Cord, but the loud clicks of cocking hammers caught their attention, stopping them. They looked to the source of the sound, saw Tabby holding the double-barreled coach gun and a grin.

She shook her head and said, "If you want to pick up that trash and take him outta here, go ahead. But keep your hands away from your weapons or this shotgun'll blast your heads off!"

Cord grinned, dropped his hands and walked slowly back to where Tabby stood beside the hitchrail that held his duster and pistol belt, wincing with every step, rubbing his shoulders and upper arms that had taken the brunt of the impact of his brief imitation of a wounded crow.

Cooky came close, shook his head as he looked at Cord and said, "I thought you were dead when that man came at'chu!"

"What man? That wasn't a man, that was a rogue grizzly bear!" declared Cord, shaking his head and rubbing his bruises.

23

DIRECTION

His back was a mess of welts, bruises, scrapes and cuts. But that was just the surface, every muscle hurt and it felt as if most of his bones were broken. He lay on his stomach, stripped to the waist, legs uncovered, and Tabby sat on the bedside, rubbing their salve into the sores and massaging the swollen muscles and more. Cord moaned with every touch, but he knew it was necessary. He mumbled into his pillow, "Am I dead yet?"

"No, and you're not allowed to die! Not yet, anyway," answered Tabby. "And if you don't quit talking like that, I'll forget I'm supposed to be tender as I do this!"

"If that's your idea of tender, please don't get mad at me," answered Cord, trying to laugh, but even that hurt.

"Have you decided what's next?" asked Tabby, almost afraid of his answer.

"Well, if I ever get to where I can move, maybe it'd be best to get out of this part of the country, find someplace new."

"Any place in particular?" asked Tabby, still working on his wounds.

"I been thinkin' 'bout finding Preacher Dyer. I've told you about him before, and I thought it'd be good to see him, have a little talk with him. You know, somebody that knows the Bible and what's been goin' on in my mind, yours too, about vengeance and such."

"Where would we find him?"

"If we go back through Breckenridge, talk to the sheriff there about the Red Legs and such, then go on o'er to Fairplay, I'm sure we'd find somebody that would know his whereabouts."

"I'm game. It'd prob'ly be good to talk to somebody like that. Even though our chase is pretty much over," surmised Tabby, finishing her ministrations to the bruised and battered body before her. Yet at that thought, both remembered Moses and his two friends, Chauncey Tittle and Sam Wright, both suspected of being with the Red Legs at the same time as Newt Morrison and the others. Cord still had warrants for the three men as mentioned by the former sheriff, Byron Steele.

"Well," began Cord, "since it's a good day's ride to Breckenridge, how's about we wait till in the mornin' and get an early start?"

"Suits me. You gonna be up to goin' to the Chop House to have supper?"

"Prob'ly, long as I get up and move around a little and don't stiffen up. You might hafta come back and give me some more ointment and such," chuckled Cord as he struggled to sit up in the bed.

"Well...the clerk told me about their bath, and I was thinkin' about getting a nice hot bath. You might do well with a nap, and I'll go to my room after the bath and get all cleaned up, then I'll come get you and we can go to supper!" she smiled as she stood to leave. She turned back to Cord, smiled again, and shook her finger at him. "You mind your nurse now, understand?"

Cord chuckled, leaned forward and grabbed the pillow from behind him and started to throw it at her, but she pulled the door shut behind her, laughing as she entered the hallway. Cord twisted around, trying to stretch his sore muscles. He stood up beside the bed, did some more twisting and turning, bent over, and more, trying to shake off the hurts and finally gave up. He stretched out on the bed and fluffed his pillow, rolled to his side, and did his best to get some rest.

━━━━━━

THE SUN WAS warm on their backs as they followed the Snake River west. It was a clear day and the blue sky was void of clouds and the cool air of autumn brushed against their faces. The aspen that showed in the gulches and gulleys that scarred the mountainsides were now splashed with golden hues to contrast with the deep green and black of the thick timber. High up on the mountains where timberline forbid any trees, tiny white spots told of gamboling mountain sheep and leftover glaciers.

It was a beautiful day, and they rode side by side, often pointing out touches of high-country magnificence that both appreciated and enjoyed. The east-bound stage rumbled toward them, and they moved to the side of the road for the six-up team and the rocking coach to have the road. The shotgunner waved, the driver shouted to his team and cracked the whip over their heads, nodded to Cord and Tabby, and passed the travelers, leaving only a drifting cloud of dust to cause Cord and Tabby to duck their heads and lift their neckerchiefs to cover their nose and mouth.

As the rumble and rattle of the stage grew distant, the two travelers had resumed their ride. The stage road had kept to the north side of the Snake until the confluence with the North Fork of the Snake, and it crossed to the south side as the river pushed toward the lower hills and the wider valley. As the road crested a slight rise, they overlooked the wide valley that held the confluence of the Snake and the Blue Rivers. Cord motioned to a clearing that was shadowed by a cluster of aspen and said, "How 'bout we stop, rest the horses, have some coffee, maybe somethin' to eat?"

Tabby smiled, nodded and followed as they left the road to go to the clearing above the meandering Snake River. It was shady and offered a previously used rock circle for a fire, and as they stepped down, Cord offered, "I'll take care of the animals if you want to get some coffee goin'." Tabby nodded and dug out the coffee pot from the packs, and walked to the fire ring. There was a scattering of kindling and branches, enough for a small fire, and she soon had the fire going, the water heating, and the coffee ready for the pot.

Cord joined her on the grey log, sat close beside her and said, "So, whaddya think?"

"About what?"

"You know, about our trying new country, maybe changin' our ways, focus on living instead of killing, all that..." he shrugged.

"I think we're doing the right thing. Although, there's still others, but at least those that we were intent on bringing to justice, have been. So, I reckon it's time for us to look to our own lives."

"Yeah. I was thinkin' 'bout sendin' this,"—he pulled the marshal badge from his pocket—"back to Marshal Shaffenburg. But...I still have these," and pulled the remaining warrants from his duster pocket. "These are for those three men we left back at Montezuma. I don't think they were with the band when they hit our farm, I don't remember seein' a big

Black man, at least. But as for the other two, they did not look familiar. I got their names from Steele when he was sheriff and thought I was one of 'em."

"Well, let's just wait on that. Maybe after we talk to the preacher, he might have somethin' to say that'll help us," suggested Tabby.

Cord nodded, replaced the warrants, stood up and twisted around, stretching his sore muscles, and winced as he moved. He looked at Tabby shook his head, "I'll sure be glad to get to Breckenridge, get us a couple rooms at the hotel and have a good night's rest."

"Ummhmm, but we're goin' on to Fairplay tomorrow, aren't we?"

"Yup," answered Cord, sitting back down on the log, handing the bag of coffee to Tabby to put some in the pot.

Their ride into Breckenridge was not nearly as noticeable as the last time when they rode in with a string of horses carrying dead bodies. They passed the many storefronts and other buildings on the main street with people walking on the boardwalks and were scarcely noticed. When they reined up at the sheriff's office, they both stepped down and walked into the office, were greeted by the sheriff and offered a seat.

"Well, Marshal Beckett, it's good to see you again. And this is...?" he questioned as he motioned to Tabby.

Cord grinned, "Oh, she acts as my deputy ever

now and again. This is Tabitha Townsend, a good friend." Cord reached into his duster pocket, withdrew the warrants, and explained, "These are all that's left of those I picked up from you. Although those men are still in Montezuma, I don't think they'll be there long. The leader of the bunch might be convinced to change his ways." Cord lay the warrants on the sheriff's desk and looked up at the man.

"I see, I see. Well," began Sheriff Packer as he pushed the warrants back toward Cord, "since those came from the Territorial Marshal, and you're a deputy marshal, I think you best keep them or send them back to him."

Cord nodded, retrieved the warrants and put them in his pocket. The sheriff looked up at him and asked, "And the other warrants? Did you get the men named in them?"

Cord nodded, rose, and explained, "We did. Not by choice, but out of necessity. They were trying to kill us and we weren't quite ready for that, so we dealt them another hand and they lost."

The sheriff grinned, nodded and stood, extending his hand to Cord. "Will you be in town long?"

"No, just passing through. Headin' south for a spell," answered Cord, intentionally giving a rather vague answer. "We'll spend the night at the hotel, then headin' out in the mornin'."

THEY WERE on the trail at first light, heading south out of Breckenridge, taking the stage road that would take them to the area of Buckskin, Montgomery, and eventually to Fairplay. Tabby asked, "You seemed kinda anxious to get out of town, something wrong?"

"Didn't like the way the sheriff was inquiring as to our plans. Sometimes it's best for others not to know. It's probably nothing, but I got to thinkin'. Today's Saturday, and tomorrow is Sunday and that might be the best time to find Preacher Dyer. He usually preaches in Fairplay and other places, so..." he shrugged, grinning.

24

FAIRPLAY

THEY TRAVELED THE STAGE ROAD FROM BRECKENRIDGE, heading ever up into the higher mountains always bound to the south and following the Blue River upstream to its origin. The long valley of the Blue River lay in the shadows of the massive mountains some were calling Ten Mile Range on the west and Hoosier Ridge on the east. Few hillsides had been missed by the many prospectors, always digging holes, leaving ore dumps, searching for the gold that would fulfill their dreams, yet leaving behind scarred mountains.

It was nearing midday when the rattle of trace chains, the rumble of wheels and the shouts and whip-cracking of a driver shattered the quiet of the morning as an overloaded stage came from behind them. Cord and Tabby nudged their mounts off the edge of the road and the six-up team dragged the stage up the increasing pull of the road that climbed before them. The stage was loaded with six men on top, nine inside, and the driver and shotgunner or messenger in the boot. The stage dragged a rolling cloud of dust behind it as Cord and Tabby lifted their neckerchiefs to cover their noses and mouth, turned the heads of their mounts away and shrugged deep into their dusters, to let the cloud pass over.

They caught up with the stage at the crest of Hoosier Pass. The stage had stopped to give the horses a breather and the passengers a break for a walk in the trees. Cord and Tabby stopped at the edge of the trees for the same reasons, but they built a little fire for some coffee and to warm up the left over biscuits and bacon.

One of the passengers ambled over, nodded and spoke, "Looks like you're fixin' some coffee?"

"That's right, it'll be a while, but we've got some time," drawled Cord, knowing the man was wanting some coffee, yet knowing the stage would not wait long before pulling out. He noticed the man's city-slicker attire, grinned and asked, "Goin' to Fairplay on business?"

"Ummhmm, lookin' to start a bank there. What with all the gold hunters around there and other places, should be a good place for a bank." The man slipped his thumbs behind his galluses, leaned back to show his brocade vest that stretched across his ample middle. He put on his best grin, "You goin' to Fairplay? If so, you might have need of a banking establishment."

Cord shook his head, "No, just passin' through. Don't know where we'll end up, but..." he shrugged, glancing up at the man.

The stage messenger called out, "Get aboard, folks! We need to get goin'!"

The banker turned slightly, looked at the coffee pot as it began to dance, shook his head and tipped his hat to Tabby, and grumbled as he returned to the stage. Once everyone had clambered back aboard, the driver cracked his whip, shouted at the six-up of mules, and they leaned into their traces, rocked the stage, making all those up top to grab the luggage rails, and the stage rolled away. Cord and Tabby watched, and Cord chuckled, "that banker sure was wantin' some coffee!"

"We coulda given him some," answered Tabby, looking at Cord with a questioning expression.

"Bankers never give hand-outs, why should we?"

As they started from their noon break they passed a sign at the crest of the pass with one board pointed north and read *Breckenridge,* another with an arrow pointed south that read *Montgomery, Buckskin, Alma, Fairplay.* But someone had drawn a line through Montgomery and Buckskin. Those had already become ghost towns when the gold was gone. Fairplay and Alma still had residents, most of whom were gold hunters. Alma was just a little over five miles, but they were in no hurry and ambled along. The stage road hugged the west edge of the valley of the Middle Fork of the South Platte River, staying near the tree line on the west bank. As they neared the town, the road crossed the river, and the town lay in the shelter of the east hills. The town of Alma was a typical gold rush town, a smattering of buildings scattered about with most on the west side of the road. There were several log cabins, some already boarded up, a few with clapboard siding, two or three business buildings with false fronts, and a couple two storied buildings, one with *Hotel* painted across the front. But they had no need of supplies and rode on through town, a few people on the boardwalks looked their way, one lazy dog lifted a disinterested wrinkled face their direction, but soon dropped his chin to the boards.

As they rode from Alma, the road again crossed the river, pointed to a low saddle of the west hills, and climbed into the timber. They passed another of the common signs that told of Fairplay being four miles away. Once over the saddle between the timbered hills, the road dropped into the valley of Beaver Creek, turned downstream and took them into the town of Fairplay. They soon found a hotel, and after securing a couple rooms, Cord found a livery for the animals.

They had settled into their rooms, and after a knock on the wall, Tabby came from her room to meet Cord in the hall. She frowned as he came from the room, grinning. He looked at her, "Ready to go get somethin' to eat?"

"I'm always ready to eat, at least when I don't

hafta cook!" she declared with a smile. They started toward the stairs and Tabby led the way. As she dropped to the first stair, a voice called out from behind them, "Is that Cordell Beckett?"

Cord turned to see Pastor Dyer, coming from the opposite end of the hall, grinning ear to ear and with a hand outstretched. Cord smiled, reached out his hand to shake with the preacher. "Pastor Dyer, fancy meeting you here!" he declared as they shook hands, grinning at one another. Tabby had stopped and looked back and Cord turned, "Pastor, I want you to meet Miss Tabitha Townsend, Tabby."

The preacher moved closer, nodded to Tabby, "Pleased to meet you, miss. Are you traveling with this man?" he asked.

"Yessir, we've been on a, well, I guess you could say, sort of a mission, together." She smiled and turned back to make her way down the stairs, leading the men to the lower floor. As they came to the foyer, she turned, looked at the Pastor, "Actually, we came here to see you, Pastor. Would you have dinner with us?" she asked.

"Certainly. I'd love to dine with you, after all me and this young man have been through, I'd like to hear about your mission."

———

NEXT DOOR TO THE HOTEL, the Summer Restaurant was the most popular in the growing town and several were already seated when the three entered, but the pastor motioned to a table in the corner, and Tabby led the way. A young man with a stained apron came to their table, a broad grin as he looked at Tabby, then asked, "What can I do for you folks this fine day?"

"What's the special?" asked the preacher.

"We have fresh beef roast with all the trimmin's," he declared, nodding to one and all.

The preacher looked to Cord and Tabby, received smiles and nods, and turned to the waiter, "We'll have that, then, please."

"For everyone?" he asked, looking at the others, lingering on Tabby.

Everyone nodded, Cord chuckled and glanced to Tabby and back to the preacher. Pastor Dyer turned to Cord, "So, what have you been doing since we were last together?"

Cord dropped his eyes, looked back up to the preacher, "Same as always, preacher. Trackin' down the vermin that were part of the Red Legs, bringing 'em to justice."

The pastor frowned, "I thought you'd be done with that by now."

Cord dropped his eyes, but continued to tell about the hunt for the outlaws and the subsequent happenings. He explained about the gang attacking the claim of the Townsend's, killing Tabby's brothers, their capture of Tabby, and more. "And that's why Tabby has been with me, and been a part of that hunt."

Tabby leaned forward to add, "And that's why we're here, Pastor. We came especially to find you, talk to you and get some guidance about, well, our future."

Pastor Dyer looked from one to the other, and with a questioning look to Cord, he nodded for Cord to add to Tabby's comment.

"That's right, Pastor. We're tired of huntin' and killin', and thought we'd try to leave it in the Lord's hands and maybe get a fresh start." He glanced from the pastor to Tabby and back, "That's why I wanted to talk to you about me'n Tabby getting married."

Tabby jerked as if she had been slapped, she leaned back, looked hard at Cord, glanced to the pastor and back to Cord, "Uh, that's the first I've heard about that!" but she relaxed into a broad smile, sat forward and reached out to touch Cord's hand that rested on the table. Before more could be said, the young man brought their food, setting three plates down, returned for more and brought cups, coffee, and biscuits.

Tabby was staring at Cord, smiling happily and glanced to a grinning Pastor Dyer. The pastor said, "Well...how 'bout we ask the Lord's blessing on our supper, then we can talk about the rest later."

25

SERVICE

CORD AND TABBY WALKED HAND IN HAND AS THEY CAME TO the church building. Pastor Dyer had told them the people of Fairplay had gone to Montgomery, taken down this log building that had been a hotel in Montgomery, hauled it down to Fairplay and reconstructed it for a church. This was to be the first service in the building, and Pastor Dyer was excited about what had been done. He stood at the door, welcoming everyone into the building and smiled broadly when Cord and Tabby approached. "Well, good morning my friends. It is so good to see you this day, and don't forget, we're having a picnic on the grounds as a celebration of this new building and you're invited to stay!"

"Thank you, preacher, we'll do that, and we do want some time afterward if that's alright?" responded Cord, his hand still clasped in the parson's hands.

"Of course, of course. Perhaps we can sit together as we eat," he offered, nudging Cord into the building as others waited to enter. As everyone shuffled around, finding a place to sit on the several benches and few chairs, there were several men that stood along the side walls. Pastor Dyer stepped behind the pulpit, lifted his arms, "Welcome, everyone, welcome! It is so good to have so many here on this, the Lord's Day, in our new church. Now, let us bow our heads in prayer." He spoke a prayer of thanksgiving for God's blessings and this day and the many people that had come out to worship and more. When he concluded with an *"Amen!"* he looked at the woman who sat on the small bench before the new Mason and Hamlin organ-harmonium. With a nod, she began to play, *Praise to the Lord, the Almighty,* and the pastor led the singing as they started with the words, *Praise to the Lord, the Almighty, The King of creation! O my soul, praise Him, for He is thy health and salvation.* With a short pause, and another nod to the organist, they began singing, *He leadeth me, O blessed thought! O words with heav'nly comfort frought!* And the last hymn was *Jesus Loves Me, this I know, For the Bible tells me so...* The pastor nodded to the organist who rose and went to her husband's side and was seated on the bench. The pastor motioned for everyone to be seated and opened his Bible as he stated, "This morning, I take my message from Mark 12:30-31, *And thou shalt love the Lord thy God with all thy heart, and with all thy soul, and with all thy mind, and with all thy strength: this is the first commandment. And the second is like, namely this, Thou shalt love thy neighbor as thyself. There is none other commandment greater than these."*

He stepped away from the pulpit, looked at the crowd and began with, "Those are some pretty strong words. Love. Now, that's not just a warm fuzzy feeling you get when you look at your husband or wife or even your girlfriend. Love is defined in John 3:16 with one word, *gave*. Love is self-sacrifice..." he went on to expound on that thought, explaining how one who loves always puts the one loved before them. Meeting their needs first, and more. But when he spoke about *love thy neighbor*, folks began to squirm, especially when he said, "If we have more of that, most towns could retire their sheriffs and turn the jails into stores!" He chuckled, looked around, "Now, the only way you can do all that, is if you have Jesus as your Lord and Savior. That means there has to be a time in your life when you understand you are a sinner, that there's a penalty of death for that sin, and the only way out is to accept the gift of eternal life paid for by Jesus on the cross. Otherwise, you're bound for an eternity in hellfire!" He growled and scowled at the crowd when he spoke of Hellfire, and many dropped their eyes, shifted on their seats and squirmed as they stood. He continued, "But if Christ lives in you, you'll find it easier to love Him and to love your neighbor, because God is love! Amen!?" Several answered with *"Amen!"* and he said, "Now, let's bow our heads, and as Hilda plays *Home of the Soul,* I want any of you who want to come to the Lord and receive his gift of eternal life, to come forward and we'll pray together."

As the song played and a few sang the words, *I will sing you a song of that beautiful land, The faraway home of the soul...*several stepped out and made their way to the altar beside the pulpit, and the pastor accepted each one, prayed with each one, and dismissed the others.

The talk around the tables was light-hearted, even jovial and most seemed to be quite happy. Another couple joined Cord and Tabby, introduced themselves as William and Winnie McCorkle.

"But folks just call us Bill and Win," explained the smiling red-faced man. He had bushy red hair, wind-burned face that gave him the appearance of always being embarrassed, and Winnie showed a bashful smile as she held her hand atop her very swollen belly.

"You folks new to Fairplay?" asked Bill as they placed their plates on the table and seated themselves.

"Oh, more or less, just passing through. I knew Pastor Dyer from before, and we stopped to talk and enjoy the services," explained Cord, lifting the coffee cup for a sip.

"Have you folks been married long?" asked Winnie, giving another coy smile to Tabby.

"Oh, we're not married, but just last night, Cord

asked Pastor Dyer about us getting married," giggled Tabby, "and that was the first I heard of it!"

Before Winnie could give a response, Pastor Dyer stepped close, looked around the table and asked, "Room for one more?"

"Of course, Pastor, please join us," offered Cord.

The conversation around the table was mostly about the town, their plans, and life on the frontier. Another woman was busy behind the tables when Winnie spotted her and turned to Bill, "Bill, I need to talk to Clarissa, she said she had some baby things for us."

Bill glanced to the table, looked at his wife and with a nod, added, "And I need to talk to Fred about his rocker box." He looked at the others at the table, "If you folks will excuse us..."

"Of course, go ahead. It's been good getting acquainted," answered Cord.

As plates were emptied and the coffee pot passed around, the pastor looked to Cord and Tabby, "So, you wanted to talk about?"

"Well, a couple things, preacher. First, about us getting married, and the other is maybe getting some counsel about leaving our hunt behind."

Preacher Dyer nodded, dropped his eyes and paused for a moment, then looked up at Cord and Tabby, "Cord, you and I have talked about this before, but I need to ask Tabby..." he turned to face her and continued, "Tabby, if you were to die today, do you know for sure that you would go to Heaven?"

Tabby frowned, looked from the preacher to Cord and back. "I think so, I mean, I believe in God and Jesus and the Bible, so I believe I would."

The pastor looked around, saw an apple sitting in the middle of the table, undoubtedly taken by someone for their desert. He nodded to the apple, "Do you believe that's an apple?"

She frowned again, "Well, of course."

"Do you believe that apple is sweet?"

"Yes."

"But do you *know* it's sweet?"

"Well, I believe it is."

The pastor nodded, "But you don't *know* if it is or not. What do you have to do to change that belief into *knowing?*"

"I guess I have to take it and taste it."

"Right. You have to put your belief into doing and change it to *knowing.* You see, Tabby, that's where a lot of people miss out. They take their believing only so far, they never take a bite of the apple so they would know if it's sweet. It's the same with our relationship with God. We can believe, think, and more, but until we put our belief into reality, we have nothing but the thin air around us. That's why it says in I John 5:13 *These things have I written unto you that believe on the name of the Son of God; that ye may know that ye have eternal life, and that ye may believe on the name of the Son of God.* Notice it says *know.*"

He continued, "But God would not tell us we could *know,* without telling us how we can know.

Now, I've kinda narrowed it down to a few things or steps for us to know for sure, and they're found in Romans. In 3:23, He says, *For all have sinned and come short of the glory of God.* We're all sinners, and because of that, we come short, or miss out on heaven. Because 6:23 says *For the wages of sin is death.* Those *wages* are what must be paid, and that's death or the grave. But he goes on, *but the gift of God is eternal life through Jesus Christ our Lord.* Notice, it's a gift. That gift is like what we said, it's more than just believing it's there, like that apple, we have to receive it. And to receive it, He tells us in Romans 10:9-13, *That if thou shalt confess with thy mouth the Lord Jesus and shalt believe in thine heart that God hath raised him from the dead, thou shalt be saved. For whosoever shall call upon the name of the Lord, shall be saved.* That's how we put our belief into action. We call upon the name of the Lord. Now, how do we call upon Him?"

Tabby seemed to relax, the wrinkles left her brow, and a slight smile tugged at the corners of her mouth, "Why, we pray."

"Right. We pray. So, the gift of God is eternal life, and all we have to do is call upon him, ask Him for it, and He will save us, save us from that penalty of death and hell forever, that's how we are saved from that, receive the free gift, and *know* that Heaven is ours forever." He paused, leaned a little closer, "Now, would you like to pray and ask for that gift?"

"Yes, yes I would. Would you help me?"

"Of course, let's bow our heads..." and Pastor

Dyer led Tabby in a simple prayer to ask for forgiveness of sin, to ask for the gift of eternal life, and to give thanks for that gift. When they finished with "*Amen*," the pastor explained about baptism. "And we're going to baptize a few others that accepted Christ as their Saviour this morning, and I'd like to see you join them."

Tabby smiled a timid smile, looked at Cord who nodded his agreement and she answered, "Yes!"

The pastor rose, announced to everyone, "Let's all go down to the river, and we'll have our baptism service!"

The crowd regathered at the river's edge, which was just below the church, and the pastor baptized four people, including Tabby, in the cold water of the Middle Fork of the North Platte River.

26

VOWS

IT WAS A SIMPLE CEREMONY. TABBY STOOD PROUD AND blushing in her borrowed wedding dress, and Cord stood proudly at her side as Pastor Dyer began to speak about marriage and its responsibilities from the fifth chapter of Ephesians in his well-worn Bible. A glance from Tabby to Winnie McCorkle brought an answering smile. She was just as bubbly and happy as Tabby as she looked back at the bride in the same wedding gown she had used just a year before. When the pastor finished telling about the responsibilities of the bride to be in submission to her husband and the husband to love his wife, he began with the vows.

"Now...Cord, repeat after me...I, Cordell, take thee, Tabitha, to be my wedded wife. To have and to hold, from this day..." And at the end of this vow, he began with Tabby's vows. Once hers were complete, he turned to Cord, nodded, and Cord lifted Tabby's hand and finished his vows with, "With this ring, I thee wed..."

As they finished, the pastor said, "I now pronounce thee husband and wife! You may kiss the bride!" And Cord happily obliged.

Winnie and William invited everyone over to their home, which was just around the corner from the church, "And we have some freshly baked wedding cake to share with everyone!" proclaimed a giddy Winnie. The *everyone* was no more than the two couples and the pastor.

———

AFTER AN EARLY BREAKFAST at the Summer Restaurant, Cord and Tabby rode from Fairplay, bound over the mountains to Oro City. Cord explained, "Before I went to Blackhawk, the man responsible for me becoming a deputy was over in Oro City, Cracker Tibbs. He is a good friend and a wise one. I'd kinda like to see him again. And Oro City might be a good place to look over, see if we want to settle there. If not, we could spend the winter, then look elsewhere."

"We're not gonna sleep out in the trees durin' winter, are we?" asked Tabby, looking around at the signs of fall with quakies shaking their leaves of gold at them.

Cord chuckled, "No, absolutely not! And even if we wanted to, Oro City is not where you want to be outside in the winter! We'll probably find a cabin some gold hunter left behind, or even build one of our own. There might even be an empty house or two in town. We'll find something suitable for our new home."

"Good, cuz me'n cold weather are not the best of friends!" declared Tabby.

They returned to the road north out of Fairplay, taking the same stagecoach road that would lead to Alma, but before they reached Alma, they turned up the meandering Mosquito Creek Gulch that would take them to the west toward the long line of granite-tipped peaks that rose well above timberline. As they entered the canyon, Cord pointed out, "Those cabins yonder, used to be the town of Mosquito, some called it Sterling. Over the hill there,"— pointing to the low ridge of rock and sparse timber that sided the Mosquito valley—"was Buckskin, and across the valley there was Park City. Musta been hoppin' in their day, but now they just look like a log cabin graveyard."

"There's a lot of places like that throughout these mountains, aren't there," asked Tabby, frowning at the thought of hundreds if not thousands of prospectors and others covering these hills, all searching for gold.

"Ummhmm, and the most that remains of so

many are broken down cabins that used to be tall green trees, and of course, each town had its boot hill. Sad, really. All those that came were full of hopes and dreams and so many died penniless."

"That's why I'm glad you're not a prospector. Although when my brothers were doin' it, I shared their dreams. But we had so little to hang our hopes on, it seemed the only way that we could get anything. But..." she shrugged, remembering the attack by the outlaws that killed both her brothers, leaving her without any family.

"Well, we need to push on, after we get to the head of this gulch, we start climbin' to go over Mosquito Pass, and I'd like for us to get on the other side 'fore dark."

"Lead the way, my husband!" declared a smiling Tabby, proud of her man who was now her husband.

The slope of the long ridge on their right was ablaze with golden-hued aspen, the deep green of spruce and fir intermingled, but provided only a contrast of the beautiful gold of the quakies that fluttered their leaves with the slightest breeze. The further west they rode, the shoulders of the mountains pushed closer, the steep talus slopes of the mountain peaks on the left were bordered by aspen, and the higher they climbed, the smaller the aspen and more faded the colors. The thicker timber of the pines showed many avalanche and rock slide troughs that split and lined the mountain shoulders. Before them, the aspen groves showed splashes of orange amidst the gold, and all lay in the shadow of the towering peaks. On their left, rugged shoulders of granite and limestone formations were tinted with the green of mountain mosses, while a long line of black timber rode the stones like a fringed border that lay in the shadow of the bare granite faces that held a dusting of white, the early snows of high altitudes warning of soon coming winter.

The tall butte of the mountain some had called London mountain stood to mark the dividing of two gulches, one holding Mosquito Creek and the stage road that was bound for Oro City, while the other gulch pushed between two intimidating peaks, but lured prospectors into the bare and empty gulch that had no outlet. Cord and Tabby stayed on the stage road, although calling it a road was a bit of an exaggeration.

As they neared the headwaters of Mosquito Creek, the road bent to the west-southwest and began to climb across the face of the shoulder of the mountain, to angle across the side of a long razorback ridge. When they crossed the ridge, they looked to the right, where the road hugged the steep talus slope, with a narrow road that pointed to the west before turning south to cross the bald face of the higher ridge that held the crest of Mosquito pass.

Cord wanted to stop on the crest, but the cold winds forced them to keep moving. Once over the crest, the road did another hugging of the west-facing slope of the mountain, but once over the crest, the wind faded, and Cord stopped. Tabby came alongside and they sat side by side, leaning on the pommels of their saddles, looking at the green valley below. Just below them, the lower hills were colored with golden aspen, while the bottom of the distant valley showed green. Beyond the valley were the black and gold skirts of the long mountain range that carried the tallest mountains in all of the Rocky Mountains, the Sawatch Range. It was along the crest of this range that the Continental Divide marched north to south to divide the flows of the rivers of the mountains, sending those on the east to the Atlantic and the west to the Pacific.

As they came into the timber-covered ridges that sided Evans Gulch, Cord pushed into the trees that stood above the gulch bottom, and offered shade and grass for the horses. As they stepped down, Cord said, "How 'bout you gettin' us a little fire goin' while I take care of the horses. They been workin' hard and I'm gonna strip the gear from 'em, let 'em have a roll, get some graze and water at the little creek yonder. Then we might just have a bit to eat, some coffee, and maybe even a little nap!" He chuckled as he loosed the latigo and pulled his saddle and blanket off Kwitcher. He did the same for Tabby's mare, and the mule, and the animals were soon lazily grazing on the tall grass in the shadow of the trees.

Cord sat on the uphill side of the fire as Tabby

tended the coffeepot, and with arms rested on his knees, he pushed his hat back, looked up and down the gulch, and said, "Those aspen sure are pretty! Almost as pretty as my new wife!"

Tabby turned toward him with a broad smile, "Well, my husband. I don't think you're very pretty, but I sure do like the way you look and the way you talk!" She brought him a cup of steaming coffee, handed him the bag of smoked elk meat, and sat beside him, bumping him with her hip to get as close as possible.

"Whoa, you're gonna make me spill my coffee!" he declared, holding the cup out before them as he laughed and looked at his wife beside him. She giggled, "So, which is more important, the coffee or having your wife *close?*"

"Hmmm, let me think!" He frowned.

"Talk like that and you won't get any more coffee!" she declared, laughing.

———

THEY RODE into Oro City from the east, riding through Evans Gulch, Little Stray Horse Gulch, and into town. The stage road was not used as often as in the past when the stage traveled every other day, now it was more of a weekly run. Although the road was used by freighters and more, they had traveled the entire length without seeing another person.

As they came into town, Cord reined up in front

of the Mercantile, stepped down, and with Tabby at his side, walked into the store. He was greeted by Mike Densmore, the owner, with, "Well, look who's here! If it ain't Cordell Beckett, or should I say, Marshal Cordell Beckett?" He stepped around the counter, hand extended to greet Cord, and glanced at the one beside him, "And who do we have here?"

Cord chuckled, "Mike, this is my wife, Tabitha! Tabby, this is Mike Densmore, owner of this mercantile." Tabby smiled, nodded, as Mike and Cord shook hands.

Cord asked, "Seen Cracker lately?"

"I have, it was just a while ago, and I don't think he made it outta town yet. Probably over to the waterin' hole!" he chuckled, referencing the Eureka Tavern, just down the street.

"Well, I think we'll get us a room at the hotel, put our animals in the livery, and if you see him before we do, let him know we're in town," stated Cord.

"We'll see you later? Or tomorrow?" asked Mike.

"Of course, or you could find Cracker, meet us at the restaurant next to the hotel and we'll have supper together!"

"Now, that's an idea I like!" declared Mike. "I'll be closin' up here in just a little while, and I'll see if I can find Cracker and we'll meet you there in, 'bout an hour?"

Cord nodded, and with Tabby at his side, left the mercantile to get them a room and tend to the animals. Tabby carried her warbag and rifle as she climbed the stairs to their room. Cord took the animals to the livery and would return shortly. She was happy, remembering Cord had signed the register as Mr. and Mrs. Cordell Beckett. She liked that, especially knowing they would be together always.

27

ORO CITY

THE MENU OF THE ORO CITY RESTAURANT OFFERED A variety of meats, with the day's special being roast quail served with a light gravy. Second to that was rattlesnake, or Rocky Mountain chicken. The sides were potatoes, onions, carrots. Cord and Tabby had the quail, Mike and Cracker ordered the smothered bear steak. Tabby looked at the two men with a frown, "*Bear* steak?"

"Why shore, missy. The way Cooky makes it, it reminds me of home an' muh mama's cookin'," Cracker chuckled, a broad grin splitting his whiskers and mischief dancing in his eyes.

"Was your mother a good cook?" asked Tabby.

"Nah, she was turrible! That's why it reminds me of her!" he laughed as he reached for his coffee cup. Cracker had not changed since Cord had last visited. He glanced to Tabby to see that she was taking a long look at this mysterious man. His faded canvas trousers were held up with a pair of worn galluses that stretched over his grey homespun shirt. He had removed his floppy felt hat, but she remembered the brim at the front pinned back to the crown and giving a clear look at the whiskery face. His grey whiskers almost hid his ears, the beard covered the neck of his shirt, but when he twisted around to wave the waitress over for some more coffee, his faded longjohns showed. The sleeves were rolled up to expose most of his muscled forearms and it was easy to see, that this man, although he looked as old as the hills, might not be so old and was definitely in good shape. Broad shoulders stretched the homespun, a narrow waist told of a trim physique, and the hobnail boots, although scuffed, were in good condition. This man was more than he pretended to be, and a slow smile painted Tabby's face as she glanced toward Cord with a nod of approval for his friends.

As they waited, Cracker looked at Cord, "So, how's your hunt goin'?"

"Well," began Cord, "we bagged most of 'em," and he began to explain about the time spent on the hunt for the Jayhawkers since he left Oro City. He told of the attack in Blackhawk against Tabby's brothers and more. He continued with, "There's a few left, but I don't think they were involved in the raid on my family's farm, nor the attack on Tabby's claim. And...well, we're thinkin' 'bout puttin' that behind us, start a new life together." He smiled at Tabby and reached for her hand.

Cracker and Mike grinned, cast glances at one another, and with a nod from Mike, Cracker related the recent happenings in Oro City. Before he could finish, the waitress brought their meals and set them on the table, filled their coffee cups, and left. Cord and Tabby joined hands and bowed their heads, prompting Cracker and Mike to do the same, and Cord said a short prayer of thanksgiving that prompted *"Amen"* around the table and with broad smiles, everyone began to enjoy the repast.

As they finished and the waitress warmed up their coffee, Cracker continued, "So, we,"—motioning to Mike and himself—"and others been talkin' and as we did, we thought of you, wonderin' where you were and such, and lo and behold, you show up!"

"Why were you thinking of me?" asked Cord, frowning.

"Well, what we was thinkin'was that we needed us some law an'order 'round'chere. We done got us a building for a sheriff's office an' jail, kept the smithy busy building the cells and such, he just finished that up. An' now, we need us a sheriff!" declared a grinning Cracker with a glance to a smiling Mike.

Cord leaned forward, "You mean me?!"

Cracker grinned, nodding, "You ain't plannin' on prospectin' are ye?"

"Well, no, but..."

"Ain't no buts about it! You done said you was wantin' to return that there marshal badge to Denver City, and you ain't gonna be diggin' in the dirt like the rest of us fools, so, now that you have yourself a wife, you have responsibilities, and you need a reg'lar job, an' this'n pays good. And we even got a nice little house! It's one that a fella had built, thinkin' his wife an' family was gonna join him, but he hit it big and went back east, left this place empty!"

Cord lifted his eyebrows in a questioning expression, looked at Tabby and back to Cracker and Mike, both of whom were smiling and waiting for an answer. Cord lowered his eyes, glanced again at Tabby, who sat expressionless, "Well, that's something to think about, but...I just don't know. Would you give us a day or two to think about it?"

Cracker nodded, glanced to Mike, and back to Cord. "Sure, we can do that. Just so's you know, bein' a sheriff hereabouts won't be that hard, not like chasin' a gang of outlaws all around the country. Any of the problems about claims an' such are usually handled by Miner's Court, but anything else would be under the jurisdiction of the sheriff. And the rest of us, businessmen an' such, we'd all be behind you!"

The table had been cleared, and as they nursed their coffee, the waitress brought out slices of berry pie for everyone, and with wide eyes, they enjoyed the desert. As they rose to leave, Tabby asked Cracker, "Could I see the house sometime tomorrow?" she smiled and placed a timid hand on Cracker's arm.

Cracker grinned, glanced to Mike, and answered, "You betcha, missy. I'd be happy to show you that house!"

"Thank you, Cracker. That's awfully nice of you."

"Anything for you, missy!" declared Cracker, the red on his face showing through the splotchy whiskers.

Cord chuckled, offered his arm to Tabby, and they returned to the hotel. They entered the dark room, and Cord went to the side table that held the lamp, and by the light of the moon coming through the window, removed the chimney and lit the lamp. Tabby had already sat on the bed, smiled at Cord, and asked, "What are you thinking?"

"Oh, just thinking about the job offer and wondering what you were thinking."

"I think you'd make a great sheriff! And we could stay here, make our home here, and who knows"— she dropped her gaze in a coy manner—"maybe even raise a family!"

Cord smiled, chuckled, "Think so, huh?"

"Ummhmm." She nodded, smiling.

———

THE HOUSE WAS exceptional for the time and location. The prospector spared nothing when he had it built and it was one of the nicest, if not the nicest in town.

Two stories, two bedrooms upstairs with a deck over the downstairs porch. A nice kitchen with stove, a hand pump at the sink, and cabinets galore. The house had already been furnished and lacked nothing and Tabby was ecstatic as she walked through with Cord at her side. "I love it!" she declared, clasping her hands together as she smiled up at Cord. She stepped closer, grabbed the front of his duster and pulled him close, "So, sheriff, how 'bout you?"

"Sheriff? You already decided that, have you?" chuckled Cord.

"Whatever you decide, I'm with you, but I really do think this is an answer to prayer. You have a regular job you're already good at, a nice home, and a good place or community. Yeah, I think it's right," she smiled, tiptoed to kiss him, and with a coy smile said, "While you go talk to the men, I think I'll look for some dresses so I can look the part of a sheriff's wife!"

Cord chuckled, "You know, I'll be going to talk to Mike and Cracker, and Cracker said before he left us here at the house, that he'd be with Mike at the mercantile. And I think the only place you'll find dresses is at the mercantile. The only other store is for mining supplies and you'd look a little silly trying to cover up with anything they offer."

Tabby giggled, grabbed Cord's hand and said, "Alrighty then, let's go shopping!"

Cord laughed and followed along, still holding

Tabby's hand as they walked through the front door and onto the porch. She stopped on the porch, looked across the valley at the long line of distant peaks that had a fresh dusting of snow, and said, "Isn't it beautiful!" waving her hand across the canvas of landscape as if she painted it herself.

"God did an amazing work, alright," answered Cord. They stepped from the porch, started down the boardwalk toward the mercantile, and Cord's mind traveled back in time to the front porch of his parent's house to see the image of his father and mother sitting in ladder-back rockers, side by side, looking at their small farm and watching the children play in the yard and climbing the trees. It was a serene image, but was quickly erased by the image of the outlaws and the raid that burnt the farm and killed his family. He took a deep breath, lifted his eyes to his surroundings and said a silent prayer to ask for God's guidance and strength as they start a new chapter of their lives together.

28

SHERIFF

THE GATHERING AT THEIR NEW HOME WAS PUT TOGETHER by Mike and his wife, Mattie. It was a welcome to town and the new job for Cord and Tabby. All the business owners and many others were there and there was plenty to eat and drink for everyone. As Cord stood with Tabby at his side and looked at the crowd, he was surprised at so many people being there. Even Pastor Dyer had come over the hill and joined the crowd. The mood was friendly and jovial, until the front door slammed open and a burly-looking, whiskery-faced man stomped in, growling, "Where is he? Where's that new sheriff?"

Cord frowned and stepped forward away from Tabby, "That's me. What's the problem?"

The burly figure stepped close, looked Cord up and down, and growled, "We got us a problem, and we're countin' on you to fix it!"

"Alright, then, let's start by telling me the problem."

"It's water. Me'n muh brothers got farms in the valley an' we got crops growin' and they need water. So, we dug us some ditches from the river to the flats, turned water into 'em and been doin' that for the last two growin' seasons. But then some o' them crazy gold hunters decided they want the water for somethin' called hydraulic minin', whatever that is, an' all I know is it ain't gonna feed nobody or nuthin', but they dammed up our ditches and took the water for their doin's."

"Well, Mr. uh, what's your name, anyway?" asked Cord.

"I'm Bull Witcher, and muh brothers are Butch and Buck, we all got farms."

"Well, Bull, I'm no prospector, but I know some of the miners need water for their sluices and such, but whatever they use goes back into the river. But..." he paused, looked around the room and spotted Cracker, and motioned him over.

"Say Cracker, could you explain this hydraulic mining process, and why it requires so much water?"

"Hydraulic? Ain't nobody doin' that yet. I heard about some wantin' to get into it, but dint think anyone was doin' it."

"Well, according to Bull here, somebody's doin' it."

Cracker looked from Cord to Bull and back, "Well, it starts well upstream. They take water down a flue, and as it comes down, the flue gets smaller'n smaller, forcing the water into the pipe or hose. Then, with the nozzle, they can focus the stream of water, now comin' at considerable pressure, and they wash all the dirt down, turning it to thin mud that flows over into the sluices and catches the gold. Then the water, now mud, flows out and back into the river."

Cord nodded, thinking and visualizing what Cracker had told him, then looked at Bull, "And the problem is that you can't use the dirty water?"

"Not that so much, it's just that they take the water out upstream before our irrigation ditches and don't leave 'nuff for our irrigatin'! Even if we could use the dirty water, it's too far downstream."

"I see," stated Cord. "So, when did you and your brothers put in your ditches?"

"Last Spring, it took us about a year to get all our ditches ready, and we turned in the water at the beginning of growin' season, last year."

"And these miners just recently did their digging to take the water above your inlet?"

"Yeah, 'bout a month or two back. We noticed the lack of water, oh, 'bout the middle of June, I think it was. Took us a while to find out the problem, who dunnit, an' such. We talked to 'em about it, but they weren't willin' to fix it, said they was gonna take it anyway...said they had just as much right to the water as we did."

Cord nodded his understanding, knowing that

few people kept track of time and dates by anything but the rising and setting of the sun, the weather and temperature, and the colors of the aspen. So the middle of June would be well after green-up, with the grasses green and the aspen in full leaf. He looked at Bull, "Do you have any names of these miners?"

"Onliest one had a name they called Beans."

"Do you know where their minin' operation is?"

"Unnhnn, nope, just where they take the water. Reckon you could follow the water down..." he shrugged.

"Alright Bull, I'll ride out in the mornin', have a look-see, talk to whoever I can find, then we'll take it from there."

Bull grunted, looked around, saw the table with the food, raised his eyebrows and looked back at Cord, prompting Cord to grin and nod, giving him the implied permission to fill a plate and enjoy.

———

THE SUN WAS JUST BEGINNING to show its colors behind him as Cord rode from his home in Oro City. He felt a little lost without his ever-present companion of late, Tabby. But he smiled at the memory and the thought, saw Blue wagging his tail as he trotted on the road before him, and felt the briskness of Kwitcher's trot, who was always glad to be out of the stable and back on the trail. The road followed California

Gulch to the west, and the rising sun gave warmth to Cord's back, but as the sun lifted above the eastern horizon, it painted the tips of the mountains on the far side of the Arkansas River Valley. The mouth of California Gulch opened to the Arkansas River at the east edge of the long valley, while the west side stretched across the valley that held tall grasses and the few farms that struggled to raise crops in this forbidding high-country climate.

He reined up on a slight rise that offered a bit of a view of the wide valley. With binoculars in hand, he scanned the flats for the farms of the Witcher brothers. He spotted what he thought might be their farms. Each home marked by log cabins, barns, corrals, a few animals, and obviously different crops, although at this distance, it was hard to distinguish one from the other or to identify what was in each field. He dropped the field glasses, put them in the case and stuffed them into the saddlebags as he resumed his journey on the stage road. He had inquired of Bull Witcher as to the whereabouts of the ditches in question, and he was bound for the river where he would turn upstream to find the feeder ditches for the hydraulic mining operations. Witcher had said it would be easy, *"Our ditches are on the west, their's are on the east side."*

The sun showed its full face above the mountains on the east when Cord turned upstream alongside the Arkansas River. The brush was thick on the banks where the river had split into two streams. Serviceberry, honeysuckle, kinnikinnick, and willows were abundant and did their best to hide the stream, but the meandering river, though not much bigger than a typical mountain stream, went its way happily chuckling as it carried hopes and dreams of riches and more downstream.

As the stage road turned to the south, Cord took the crude trail that sided the river to the north. He saw several mule deer, the bucks shedding the velvet from the antlers and some hanging like strips of moss from the tines. The small bunch numbered less than half dozen, and the bucks stopped, lifted their heads and watched as Cord passed about a hundred yards away. He was not hunting meat on this trip, but he enjoyed seeing the wildlife. Blue had also stopped, one paw lifted and head held high as he looked at the deer, glanced over his shoulder at Cord, and with a wave from his master, trotted on ahead, scouting the trail.

The Arkansas River had divided into two separate branches for a stretch of about a mile before merging back together. It was just upstream of this divide that Cord came to the ditch that cut into the stream bed of the Arkansas and diverted the flow of much of the water. Although not a big ditch, it was deep enough to carry ample water, and the flow was considerable. It appeared there had been some effort at building a floodgate to control the flow, and was now shut down to prevent any water entering the ditch. But on the back side of the gate, it was evident the ditch had been used, but did not appear to have carried a lot of water or used very often. At this point, the river was no more than forty feet wide and at its deepest in the current, no more than two to three feet deep. Cord could easily see across the river bed and spotted what he assumed to be the ditches of the Witcher brothers. Those were downstream from the miner's ditch by about a hundred feet and on the downstream side of a sharp bend in the river.

The farmers had chosen the site of their ditches well, getting the benefit of the flow of water as it made its bend around the point of land. The miners had dug their ditch along a straight stretch of the river and had to divert the flow of water with a makeshift dam of boulders, rocks and more. Cord knew he had to follow the miner's ditch to its use point to find any of the men responsible for the work, and he mounted up, reined Kwitcher around, and taking a deep breath, prepared himself for the confrontation, knowing that any effort to stifle the work of the miners in their search for gold would be at least a challenge, at most a deadly confrontation.

29

CONFLICT

"I REMEMBER YOU, YOU'RE RELATED TO NEWT MORRISON, ain'tchu?" whined the hatchet-faced, derby-wearing dealer as he shuffled the cards at the table of the Eureka Saloon. Willy Vanhorn fancied himself as a card shark, but his luck and his talent seemed to have abandoned him as the stack of chips before him was the smallest stack of all the players.

"That's right, we was half-brothers. Same ma, different pa's," answered the man across the table. He sat with his floppy felt hat pushed back on his head, thinning hair covered his high forehead, and his mottled complexion was covered with patchy whiskers. Tobacco juice had stained his chin, and a little trickle of brown drool coursed its way through the whiskers, only to be wiped off with the back of his hand. Black eyes glared from under dark brows, a long scar sliced across his left cheek and whatever had scarred his face had taken the top of his ear with it.

He added, "You rode with the Jayhawkers, din'tchu?"

"For a while, got wounded near the end, left 'em, or rather they left me behind. Your brother, say, what is your name anyway?"

"Sam Wright."

"Yeah...your brother was in that bunch that went south into Missouri after the war. Were you with 'em then?"

"Nope, I was laid up with this," he touched the long scar on his face. "After Newt an' the others came out there, I followed. Finally caught up with 'em up to Montezuma. That's where he bought it!"

"Newt?"

"Him an' most o' the others been hunted down like rats. Got shot down like a back alley dog!" growled Sam. "Been wantin' to get back at the one what done it, follered him here." He picked up the raggedy cards dealt by Vanhorn, sorted them and glanced to the dealer over the fanned cards.

"What'chu got in mind?" asked Vanhorn, having lowered his voice so only those at the table could hear.

Sam looked around at the two other players, both staring wide-eyed and leaning forward a little to be a part of the discussion. "Dunno for sure, got me'n idea or two. You?"

Vanhorn chuckled, nodded to the two others,

"Mebbe. Been cookin' on somethin'. From what I seen an' heard o' your brother, they just stormed into a place, took what they wanted, and left with dead bodies scattered. I think it's better to work smart. When anybody shows up with gold or money, they need to have a reason for it, so..." he paused, looking from one to the other, "with a good cover, we can take what we want and no one's the wiser."

"What's your cover?"

Vanhorn leaned a little closer, fiddled with his cards, looked around the table, "It's like this. The new thing in mining placer gold is to use hydraulic mining. That's where we use high-pressure water to wash the dirt down from the hillsides and into the sluices. Now, I picked up a couple claims in California Gulch, ain't got nuthin', but if we make a show of usin' hydraulic mining, then whatever gold we take from others, we'll say came from there—nobody the wiser!" he declared as he sat back, grinning.

"So, it's just you three?"

"So far, but we could use another'n," replied Vanhorn, glancing to the two on his left. They each gave a slight nod and he turned back to Sam, "so, you want in?"

"Anything that'll give me a chance at that Beckett fella!" grumbled Sam, gritting his teeth at the memory of seeing his brother buried with the others and the fight with Cordell and Moses.

———

CORD FOLLOWED the ditch from the river, saw where the flume had been narrowed, and eventually where the wooden frame had funneled the water into the tin mouth that ended in the big hose that stretched into the bottom of California Gulch and lay unused at the edge of what was apparently the claim of the miners, but no one was around. Cord stepped down to have a better look, hoping to find something that would tell the identity of the miner or miners and what they were doing or what their plans were for the hydraulic mining. Cord knew how the hydraulic mining would wash away tons of soil and cave in the banks of a gulch like this, but it did not appear much had been done. Although there were sluices set up, none appeared to have been used.

It was unusual to find a claim with no one around, although there would be times when the miner would need to go to town for supplies and such, but even then, there would be signs of use or habitation. Cord climbed the bank of the gulch, made his way to the cabin that was set back near a couple of scraggly juniper trees, and looked about as he approached. At least here, there were signs that someone was staying at the cabin. The corral behind the cabin showed fresh horse apples, scattered hay, some tack hanging on the fence, and the cabin door was unlocked. Cord knocked repeatedly on the door, and with no response, pushed the door open and looked around. With two sets of bunks, it appeared there were four men that slept here, an empty coffee pot sat on the stove, dirty tins were stacked in the tub they used for a sink, and some dirty rags that might have been some clothes were scattered about.

Cord shook his head as he went to the door, anxious to get some fresh air from outside. As he came into the light, he heard the approach of horses and some muffled voices. He stepped clear of the cabin, shaded his eyes as he looked up the gulch bank and saw four mounted men coming down the wagon road. He lifted a hand in the air, "Howdy men! You belong to this claim?"

"That's right! What're you doin' here?" growled the man in the lead. Willy Vanhorn nudged his mount a little closer, leaned on the pommel, "Folks around here don't like strangers nosin' around their claims. Gives us the right to take whatever action we think is necessary," threatened Willy, grinning. His tobacco-stained teeth looked like a picket fence that was missing every other picket, and his drooping moustache hung down both sides of his mouth. The rest of his face was covered with about a week's worth of whiskers, and his flat-brimmed hat shaded his shifty eyes. He looked to be a little bigger than average, broad-shouldered, thick chest, and maybe just a little shy of six feet, just enough so that he felt comfortable threatening anyone he thought was smaller and slower.

"So, stranger, just what do you think we oughta do 'bout you snoopin' 'round our diggin's?"

Cord grinned, pulled his duster open to show the

shiny new star he wore on his leather vest, "Maybe you could call the law? You wanna do that?"

Vanhorn frowned, twisted in his saddle as Sam Wright heeled his horse closer and growled, "That's the one I'm after. He's the one that stomped Moses!"

Vanhorn flinched, turned to look at Sam, "He," nodding toward Cord, "stomped Moses? I know Moses, he's the big colored fella, used to be a slave and he's bigger'n a mountain. That the one?"

"Mmmhumm. He got into it with that'n, tripped o'er sumpin' and when he went down, that'n kicked Moses in the face, broke his jaw, his nose, and some teeth."

Vanhorn turned back to face Cord and asked, "That right, Sheriff? You stomped our friend, Moses?"

"Not like he said, but yeah, I did that. Had to, it was either that or let that grizzly bear eat me alive!" answered Cord, letting a slow grin split his face.

"How long you been the sheriff?" asked Vanhorn.

"Long enough to be answering a complaint from the Witcher brothers 'bout you men takin' water from the river and keepin' it from their crops."

"Well now, Sheriff, as you can see, we ain't usin' no water right now!" pleaded Vanhorn.

"That's fine, but 'fore you start usin' it again, you might wanna be neighborly and check with the Witchers so they won't be without water for their crops and animals."

"Now, why would we do that? It's just water, an' we have as much right to it as they do!"

Cord slowly shook his head, "No, I don't think that's the way the judge would see it. It's like this, they were first to put in ditches, first to take water, and did not take it from anybody else that needed it at the time. So, that gives them the right of firsts. But you men came along later, put in your ditch, and when you use it, take it from them. No, I don't think the judge would see it your way."

30

RETALIATION

CORD RETURNED TO KWITCHER, MOUNTED UP, AND WITH A glance toward the cabin, rode away from the claim. He had recognized Sam Wright and was surprised to see him here in Oro City. He had hoped they left the memory of the Jayhawkers or Red Legs behind when he and Tabby had come over the mountain to start a new life.

It was a short jaunt back to town and he reined up in front of the new sheriff's office, grinning as he stepped down and slapped the reins over the hitch rail and stepped up onto the boardwalk. He pushed open the door and was surprised to see Tabby sitting in the chair behind the desk, smiling broadly and laughing at his expression as she greeted him, "Well, howdy sheriff! How'd your first day on the job go so far?"

Cord chuckled, pulled up the chair that sat at the wall and sat down in front of the desk, put his elbows on the desktop and looked at his smiling wife, "Well, howdy deputy! How'd your first day in town go for you?"

Tabby stretched across the desk and planted a kiss on Cord's lips, then sat down with a smile. "Oh, it was o.k., but I was feelin' a little lonesome. How 'bout'chu?"

Cord chuckled, dropped his eyes, "Not quite how I'd like, but...ran into someone I didn't want to see."

Tabby frowned, leaned on the desk and looked at Cord, "Who?"

"Remember those two that were with the big colored fella, Moses?"

Tabby frowned, remembering, "Uh, yeah."

"One of them. The one with the scar on his face. He's mixed up with the miners that are wantin' to do hydraulic mining, taking water from the Witcher brothers."

"That's not good. What're you gonna do?"

"We wanted to put that vengeance hunt behind us, but I think this one, and maybe the others were with the Jayhawkers too."

"But it's got to stop somewhere, isn't that what Preacher Dyer said?"

"Yeah, but I can't let my guard down." He looked around, thinking, looked back at Tabby, "Reckon we'll just take it one day at a time."

"Ummhmm, and as long as we're together, you, me and Colt can handle anything!" She patted her

Colt that sat in the holster on her hip and grinned at Cord.

———

CRACKER STEPPED into the sheriff's office, grinning from ear to ear and laughed when he saw Cord leaning back in his chair, his feet on the desk and his hands clasped behind his head. "Well, if you ain't the picture of small town sheriff!"

Cord slowly grinned, sat up and put his elbows on the desk and gave a serious frown as he looked at Cracker, "And just what is the problem, Cracker? Got a complaint for the sheriff, somebody need to be put in jail, want me to arrest somebody, maybe shoot somebody?" he chuckled.

Cracker pulled a chair up in front of the desk, sat down and crossed his arms over his chest and asked, "What's happenin' with the Witcher brothers' water problem?"

Cord gave Cracker a brief rundown of his confrontation with the men on the claim and the progress of their hydraulic operation. "But I don't think they'll really be doing any hydraulic mining. None of 'em look to be the type to do any real work, somethin' just doesn't look right, and with at least one of 'em bein' former Jayhawkers, well..."

"Jayhawkers? I thought you were done with that," answered Cracker.

"Thought so, but the one I recognized was from

the bunch o'er in Montezuma. I'm thinkin' he followed me here. But why? I don't know."

"So..." drawled Cracker, frowning and thinking, "how many were there in Montezuma?"

"When we first got there, we met some we did not know about, including the self-appointed sheriff, and he had seven or eight with him. Our first encounter took care of four of 'em. After that, Newt Morrison showed up and there were oh, maybe six or seven of them. But when we took care of that bunch, there were three new ones in town, one of 'em bein' the fella I saw today. The other two were more gamblers than fighters."

Tabby giggled and covered her mouth before adding, "The one *gambler* picked a fight with Cord, and I thought he was gonna get kilt, but he came out of it with a whole lot of hurtin' goin' on, but not as bad as the beast he was fighting!" she smiled at Cord to see his response.

"So, you know anything about this one, the one that's here?"

"Nope, just that he's one of the bunch from Montezuma and in my book, that makes him a Jayhawker, and chances are the three he's tied up with, were Jayhawkers as well."

Cracker slowly shook his head, wondering, "Reckon there's not much you can do until they break the law or somethin'."

"Ummhmm," mumbled Cord. "But until then, how's about we go get us somethin' to eat?" He looked from Cracker to Tabby as they both came to their feet and started to the door, supposing Cord was at their heels.

They had no sooner sat down in the café than the door slammed open and three burly men stomped in and came to the table. They grumbled as they pulled another table and chairs close, and with nothing more than a glance to Cracker and Tabby, glared at Cord. Bull Witcher growled, "Well, sheriff, what'chu gonna do 'bout our water?"

Cord doffed his hat, hung it on the post of the chair behind him, and leaned forward on his elbows, and with a glance to the brothers, looked at Bull with as stern a stare as he could muster, "I was out there this mornin' to look things over. I saw your ditches, rode upstream and saw their ditch and headgate. After I followed the ditch to California Gulch and their claim, I saw their equipment and..." he paused, leaned back. "I'm not impressed. I don't think they know what they're doin' and prob'ly won't be doin' it long. But..." He leaned forward again. "Some of those men are former Jayhawkers out of Kansas and I'm a little leery of what they have planned. Yet...I'd appreciate it if you fellas keep an eye on things and the next time you see them open their floodgates and turn water in, you hotfoot it down here and let me know. I warned them you have prior rights, and that if they took water from you, they'd have to answer to the judge."

Cracker interrupted, "Uh, Cord, the only judge is the district judge and he's down to Granite."

"He ever come up here?"

"Hasn't so far, but..." Cracker shrugged.

"Well, that's not the important thing, let's see if we can take care of it first."

"You better! Cuz if'n you don't, we'll take care of it our way, and you too!" growled Bull, nodding to his brothers as they rose and stomped from the room.

Cord watched them leave, looked at Cracker and Tabby, grinned and said, "I thought we were gonna have dinner!" and motioned the aproned cook over to the table.

———

"I WANT him to see me when I kill him!" growled Sam Wright as he looked at the others. "I'm tellin' you, if we don't take care of him and soon, we ain't gonna get anywhere with your plan of using the hydraulic mining! That's the man that killed my brother and he wiped out all those that had been ridin' with him!"

"Hold your horses! If I remember right, you and your brother didn't even like each other! Why, I remember one time when you almost killed him over some nonsense about a barfly!"

"That don't matter none! He was my brother!" retorted Sam, growling and grumbling as he stomped around the cabin, pushing and shoving everything that got in his way. "If we don't put him under, all your plans won't be worth a gob o' used tobaccy in a brass spittoon!"

Vanhorn frowned, looking at the tantrum-throwing newcomer. "I'm beginnin' to think you're afraid of him!"

"Think about it, Willy, he killed Newt and his men, stomped Moses in the dirt single-handedly, and if he ain't somebody to steer shy of, I don't know who is!"

"Alright," began Vanhorn, before looking at the other two men that had been with him for some time, and continued, "then I've an idea how we can get him out here and ambush him." Vanhorn motioned to the others, gathered them around the table and began to explain his plan. When he finished, he grinned, leaned back and said, "So, what'chu think?"

"Sounds like it'll work, but like I said, I want him to be lookin' at me when I kill him!" snarled Sam.

31

FACEOFF

WINTER WHISPERED IN DURING THE NIGHT, NO announcement, no warning, just the sudden drop of temperature from the 40s to hovering around 0°. But that was common for the high country in the Rocky Mountains, with the only warning being the changing of the colors on the quakies that splashed gold over the mountainsides, to donning the deep white of winter's coat of snow. When Cord stepped out on the porch, stretched and took a deep breath of the cold morning air, he hugged himself and shivered. As he looked at the mountains with their granite peaks tucked into the low-lying and grey-bellied clouds, he felt the cold breeze of winter on his face. With a shake to try to rid himself of the cold, he turned back into the house for some of Tabby's hot breakfast.

When he entered, she smiled and said, "I'm likin' this cookin' on a stove. Been a long time!" She nudged the coffeepot off the center trivet, pushed it toward the back. She bent to remove the biscuits from the oven, stood and opened the door to the warming oven above the burner top and placed the pan of biscuits inside. She grabbed the cast iron skillet, placed it on the center or hottest trivet, cracked two eggs in the hot grease and began frying Cord's eggs. She looked his way, smiled broadly, and turned back to her work.

Cord sat down at the kitchen table, looked out the window and said, "Winter's come. It's so cold out there I almost froze to the porch!"

"Oh, come on now. It can't be that cold! Why, the begonias were still blooming in the garden!"

"Won't anymore! At least not till next spring! I'm tellin' ya, it's colder than a witch's heart!" Cord chuckled, watching Tabby busy at being a housewife. "We'll prob'ly see a mass exodus of the placer miners. Cracker said most of 'em hightail it south when winter comes, says it's impossible to do anything without running water and a few more days of this, there won't be anything but ice in the little creeks, even the river will freeze over. He said the only miners that stay around are those doin' the hard rock mining inside the mountain, and even they slow down quite a bit."

"Then I s'pose the sheriff's job gets a little easier, doesn't it?" asked Tabby, focusing her attention on the eggs and bacon sizzling in the skillet.

Cord rose from his seat, coffee cup in hand and

went to the stove beside Tabby to pour himself a cup. He slipped an arm around her shoulders, pulled her close and said, "I hope the sheriff'n gets easier. Gives us more time together," he laughed as he returned to the table. "One thing it'll do is keep the hydraulic minin' bunch from doin' anything, and that should settle the feud between them and the Witchers." As he sat down, a thunderous knock at his front door brought him to his feet with a frown and a glance to Tabby as he started for the door.

He opened the door to see Bull Witcher stomping around on the porch, and he turned as Cord opened the door. "You said to come tell you when they started stealin' the water! An' they done it! They got that headgate wide open and rocks stacked to divert the flow and water's pourin' into that ditch o' their'n!" he growled.

Cord frowned, motioned for the man to come inside and as they stood in the entryway, Cord said, "But with the temperature as low as it is, they can't do any hydraulic mining—everything'll freeze!"

"Mebbe, mebbe not. But don't make no difference, we need to fill up our cisterns so we can have water for our stock! An' you said you'd do somethin' 'bout it!"

"Alright, alright, you go on back home, and I'll go see about the water. If you want to shut their floodgate, go ahead. I'll talk to Vanhorn and his cronies."

Cord opened the door and Bull stomped out, grumbling all the way and Cord watched as the man stomped down the walkway and grabbed the reins of his tethered horse, swung aboard, jerked the horse's head around and rode down the street to return to his home.

As Cord returned to the kitchen and the table, he watched as Tabby set a full plate before him and another for herself and seated herself opposite him. He smiled at her, took her hand and they bowed their heads for a short prayer of thanksgiving and asking for God's direction and protection for the day. Tabby lifted her head with a broad smile, looked at Cord, "Sometimes I think sheriff'n is a lot like babysitting! 'Ceptin' the babies are a bit bigger and louder, but crybabies all the way!"

"Don't let them hear you say that, you'll get an argument for sure, even if it is true!" They both laughed and focused on their breakfast, enjoying the time together that had already become Tabby's favorite time of the day.

————

CORD BUTTONED in his wool lining for his oilcloth duster, slipped it on and started for the door. "Hold on there, Sheriff! Aren't you forgetting something?" asked Tabby, standing with hands on hips and a broad smile on her face.

Cord chuckled, walked back to stand before her, smiled down and grabbed her around the waist to pull her close and lay a big kiss on her lips. She squirmed around some, but did not fight, and returned the kiss with all the ardor he offered. She pulled back, smiled up at him and said, "That's better!"

"You try to stay home today, stay out of trouble," directed a smiling Cord.

"You're the one that needs to be cautioned about getting into trouble. Even if there isn't any waiting, you'll stir things up until you find some!" She smiled at her man, enjoying the banter. "But, I might have to go see Mike at the mercantile, he said he had a couple dresses in stock that might be just my size, and seein' as how the only outfits I have are a couple split skirts and that ol' duster, I could use some new clothes. Gotta look the proper sheriff's wife, don't I?"

"Alright, alright. But if you do, you better stop by the office to see me!" ordered a smiling sheriff, turning back to the door to leave. With a wave and a word to Blue, the big dog took to his heels. Cord went to the livery instead of the office, determined to go check the water and satisfy the Witchers. They were bound and determined to get their way, probably because the three of them were the equal of any four or five other men and they had lived a life making their own way and forcing their will upon others. Cord was thinking about Bull and his brothers as he saddled the big dun stallion, stroking his neck as he talked to him, "You understand, don'tchu boy? We could handle any one of 'em, but all three at the same time? Not hardly!" Blue rubbed up against Cord's leg as Cord finished rigging the stallion. When he swung aboard, Blue ran around in a circle, barked happily, and led them out the door of the livery.

It was about a five-mile jaunt from town to the headgates of the ditch used by the hydraulic mining. As he rode from town the rising sun had crested the eastern mountains and shone warm on his back. The air was cold, his breath came in whispers of white, and the frost showed on all the grass and shrubs. The distant mountains to the west still had their heads tucked in the clouds, but the skirts of black timber were tinged in white as Jack Frost showed himself capable of having his own way wherever he chose. But it was a beautiful sight as the sun made the frost sparkle and shine, and the frosty mists rose off the warmer water. Ice showed at the edges of the little stream that twisted and turned in the bottom of California Gulch, and the world was quiet, the only sounds coming from the shod hooves of Kwitcher and his occasional snorts to clear his nostrils of accumulating frost.

Cord hunkered down into his duster, the wool scarf around his neck giving some added comfort, the felt hat shaded his eyes and kept the top of his head warm, but the cold seeped around the back of his head, his ears and his face. He chuckled to himself, *So, what're ya gonna do when it really gets cold?*

He reined up as he neared the headgate, saw the gate was still open, but no water was going down the ditch. He leaned to the side, looking a little closer, and frowned at what he saw. The rocks that had been lined out in the water to divert the flow, were gone. Either the miners did not do a very good job of building the partial dam, or the current was too great, or...the Witchers had scattered the rocks to prevent the diverting of the water, without touching the headgate. Cord grinned, saw no need of confronting the miners, but chose instead to visit the farmers.

The east side of the Arkansas River valley was bordered by a long flat-top butte that was thick with heavy timber, pines, spruce and firs. The shoulder of that butte rose above the wagon road that Cord had followed from town, but now he faced the slow-moving, shallow, meandering river that showed as much ice as water. Although only about forty to fifty feet wide and no more than knee deep on Kwitcher, it looked cold and Kwitcher balked a little, but with some urging and heels digging in his ribs, he stepped into the water, breaking the thin ice at the edges and quickly made his way across, climbing the low bank and giving a thorough shake that Cord thought would loosen the saddle. But it held, and so did Cord, and they started to the first of the Witcher homes.

Bull Witcher stood on his porch watching Cord ride up his roadway toward the log cabin house. Bull stood every bit of six feet and then some, and the low-roofed porch made him look even bigger. He hollered at Cord, "I see you made it! Step on down and come in for some hot coffee!" he ordered as he turned to enter the house.

Cord reined up at the hitchrail, stepped down, stroked Kwitcher's neck and looked at Blue, "Stay here with Kwitcher, boy." He stepped up on the porch, went to the door but it opened before he could knock, and Bull said, "C'mon in! We don't get many visitors." He turned and called over his shoulder, "Ma! Got comp'ny!" and motioned for Cord to take a seat at the table. As Cord glanced around, the house was tidy, well cared for, and with curtained windows, a round rag rug covered the plank floor, and the home was warm and cozy. Bull sat a steaming cup of coffee before him, sat down himself and looked at Cord, "So, you see the headgate?"

"I did. But it's still open, but not gettin' any water."

Bull grinned, "Yeah, I thought that'd fix 'em for a while, leastways till we get 'nuff for our stock and cisterns." He reached for his cup just as his wife came out of the back room, grabbed the coffee pot and refilled both cups. She was a portly woman, a touch of grey in her hair, and no-nonsense in her eyes as she gave Cord the once-over. She nodded as Bull introduced her. "This is muh wife, Victoria," and took a sip of his hot coffee. He watched as Cord did the same, then added, "You might wanna watch yourself, sheriff. I was 'crost the river, couldn't hear ever'thin' they said an' they din't see me, but sounded somethin' like *That'll fix him. We'll get the sheriff sure 'nuff.* No tellin' what they're up to, but might watch yourself."

Cord nodded, cocked one eyebrow up as he thought of the comment, explained, "One of the four I've seen before. He used to run with the Jayhawkers. Might have a stick in his craw 'bout somethin'," he shrugged. They finished their coffee and Cord thanked the missus, "Mighty fine coffee ma'am, thank you." She nodded as Bull followed Cord to the door.

32

SWITCH

As Cord rode back into town, he was riding thoughtful. The sun was just shy of high noon and had chased away the frost, but the leaves of the grass and bushes still sparkled with the tidbits of moisture that remained. Blue trotted ahead, tail wagging and head high. Kwitcher kept his usual ground-eating gait, his ears pricked and head high as he watched the dog and the road before them. Cord lapsed into his reverie of remembrances, thinking of his home in Missouri and his family, remembering the tragedy of the Red Legs attack, and the emotions were stirred within.

One of the men, and perhaps all four, that were a part of the Hydraulic mining operation, or what they pretended was such, had been a part of the Red Legs, although he did not believe any of them had a part of the attack on his home place, but that did not relieve them of responsibility for the many bloody attacks before and after that time. He knew the bunch that had been led by Newt Morrison and before Morrison by "*Doc*" Jennison and others, had done more than their share of terrorizing and killing prospectors, robbing stages, and more. But he also knew association does not equal guilt. He shook his head as he thought about the more recent encounter and wondered just what they had in mind with what Bull Witcher overheard about '*getting*' the sheriff.

———

"I'M TELLIN' ya! He ain't comin'! I seen him down to the headgate, he sat there lookin' around, then just up and crossed the river and headed for that Witcher place," declared Mitchell Plummer, the tallest and leanest of the four men. The only thing longer than his nose was his black hair that draped over his collar in a tangle of curls, his black eyes and thick eyebrows gave him a look like a wolverine, and his long fingernails added to that look. "Now what're we gonna do, if he ain't comin' up here, that mean we gotta go into town after 'im?"

Vanhorn looked around the dimly lit room of the cabin, Sam Wright was sitting on the edge of one of the bunks, the upper bunk shading his face. Parker Finnegan, the fourth member of the bunch, stood beside the dirty window, leaning against the logs and showing his disdain for the whole idea of waylaying the sheriff. He was a medium-built man, usually clean-shaven, dressed more like a cowboy than a miner with boots, canvas pants, leather vest over a homespun shirt and a floppy felt hat that shaded his face. He usually had a Remington pistol in his belt and a Green River knife in a scabbard on his hip, but he had recently bought a holster and belt rig that he was fidgeting with now, using the light from the window to load the loops with metal cartridges for his converted Remington.

"What do the rest of you think?" asked Vanhorn, looking around the cabin from his seat at the table. He had been playing solitaire and cheating but now sat the deck down and looked at the men.

Mitchell Plummer said, "If he's as bad as Sam says, we either gotta kill him or leave the country!"

Vanhorn glanced to Sam, and Sam spoke, "You know what I think, as long as I get my vengeance, that's all I care," he growled as he stood beside the bunk.

Vanhorn turned to Parker, who added, "Like Mitchell says, it's either kill or run, an' I ain't partial to runnin', cuz once you start, there ain't no end to it but a hole in the ground."

"Alright, then come to the table and we'll see what we can come up with. I'm thinkin' we can do 'bout the same as we had planned for here, just gotta figger out the places and such."

WHEN CORD WALKED into his office, he was surprised
to see Cracker sitting on the edge of his desk and
grinning. Cord said, "I thought you had a home
somewhere, or a cabin or somethin', you've been
hanging around town ever since I come back.
What's up?"

Cracker chuckled, "Oh, just keepin' a check on
you, makin' sure you're stayin' out of trouble."

Cord walked around his desk, doffed his hat and
hung it on the peg behind him, and sat down. He
chuckled, "I still ain't used to this chair. Seems like
ever'body else has been sittin' in it besides me!"

"Well, does it fit?" asked a grinning Cracker.

"Startin' to."

Cracker pulled up a chair and asked, "You been
out to see the Witchers?"

"Ummhmm, looked at the ditch headgate, then
went to Bull's place."

"Anything happen?"

"No, just had coffee and left. Didn't see anyone
else, but..." and he explained to his friend what Bull
had said he overheard. "Don't know what that's
about, but I'm thinkin' one of 'em was with the gang
in Montezuma. Thought we left that behind, but
maybe he's followin' me."

"Reckon it don't feel good being the object of
vengeance, do it?"

"Not even a little bit!" answered Cord, standing
to pace around the office, considering this unex-
pected change.

Cracker watched Cord pacing and thinking. He shook his head, rose from his seat and replaced the chair against the wall. He pushed his hat back away from his brow, cocked one eyebrow high and looked at Cord, "Wal, young'un, you can walk aroun' in circles till you're wore to a frazzle, but I'm goin' to muh cabin. It's on the other end o' town, an' since you ain't been there yet, if'n you decide to come or sumpin', it's the soddy with the red door, or what used to pass for red, more like rust, I reckon." He turned to the door, waved to Cord as he pulled it open and walked out.

When Cracker walked around town, he all but disappeared. He was one of the many old sour-doughs that wore canvas britches, hob-nail boots, faded red Union suit under a homespun shirt. His britches were held up by galluses, sometimes only one gallus, and a floppy felt hat. Yet the front of Cracker's hat was pinned back flat above his fore-head, giving a full view of the greying whiskers that covered his face and neck. He made it a point to walk as if bow-legged or crippled, and if noticed, he would not be considered a threat of any kind. He was one of those that was seen but went unnoticed, he was there, but he was not remembered. Yet, Cracker knew and was known by all the businessmen and successful miners and prospectors, and respected by one and all, and was, in fact, a leader of the community.

Cracker knew of his visual anonymity and took

advantage of it whenever there was something about to happen or strangers came into town. He took a seat in the shade of the porch in front of the mercantile and leaned back against the wall, his hat pulled down to almost cover his eyes. Just enough so he could see everything that was happening.

———

IT WAS MID-AFTERNOON, and the sun was high and giving the much-desired warmth to this late fall, early winter day, when four men rode into town, reined up before the Eureka Saloon, and disappeared through the swinging doors. Cracker watched, pretending to sleep, but was stirred when a woman's voice said, "Why Cracker! Whatever are you doin' on this nice day?"

Tabby grinned as Cracker dropped the chair to all fours, pushed his hat back and let a broad smile split his whiskers. He chuckled, rose to his feet and nodded to Tabby, "Why, Mrs. Beckett, I do declare. You look mighty fetchin' today!"

Tabby grinned, "Thank you, kind sir. I was just on my way into the mercantile. Mike said he had some new dresses and such that might be just my size, so..." she shrugged as she turned to the door. She paused, looked back at Cracker, "If you find yourself in need of something to do, you might come inside and give me your opinion as to my choices of new dresses." She flashed a coy smile, stepped inside and the door swung closed behind her.

Cracker returned to his seat and resumed his position and wary eye on the saloon, expecting some trouble from the four men he and Cord suspected of being former Jayhawkers and probably up to no good. Cracker had no doubt as to what was meant by the expression *to get that sheriff* that was overheard by Bull Witcher. He just hoped somehow, he could keep that from happening, or at least help Cord to even the odds or to turn the tables on the outlaws.

Cracker frowned when he saw two of the four men exit the tavern, look around, go to their horses and slip rifles from the scabbards, and started off in different directions. One, who looked more of a cowboy than a miner, started down the street on the same side where Cracker sat, but soon disappeared into the walkway between the mercantile and the café. The other, a tall, lean man whose most obvious feature was a long nose, took to the opposite side, and also disappeared into a bit of an alleyway between buildings.

Cracker did not move, nor giveaway his presence in any manner, looking like any other old sourdough taking a nap in the middle of the afternoon. Although there were a few folks in town, one with a wagon in front of the miners supply store, a few others walking the boardwalk bound to either the café, the mercantile, or the tavern. When Cracker saw the swinging doors of the tavern push open again, he saw the derby-wearing card dealer step to the edge of the boardwalk, pause with his thumbs tucked into the armholes of his vest as he looked up and down the street. It was obvious he was speaking to someone who still stood behind the doors, but were slowly pushed open to allow the one Cracker knew to be Sam Wright, come out. Both men went to their horses and withdrew their rifles, looked around and stepped back onto the boardwalk.

Cracker had seen enough and casually dropped his chair to all fours and stood, stretched, and stepped into the mercantile. Once inside, he called out, "Mike, Mike! Them outlaws are laying an ambush for Cord!"

Mike scurried from behind the counter only to see Tabby come from the back room, a new full dress on and holding a frock coat over one arm. She looked wide-eyed at Cracker, "Did you say an ambush?"

"Uh, yeah, looks like it. I reckon it's that bunch that had a run-in with the Witchers. Cord thought one of 'em might be a Jayhawker he recognized from Montezuma."

Tabby rushed to the door, looking out the window, saw a furtive figure in an alleyway across the street, looked at Cracker, "Is he one of 'em?"

Cracker nodded, "Ummhmm, an' there's anoth-er'n o'er here, and two comin' down the street."

Tabby glanced around quickly, looked at the old-timer, "Cracker! Load those Greeners, quickly!" nodding to the rack that held the Greener shotguns and other rifles. As Cracker grabbed the shotguns, Tabby slipped on the long frock coat, raised the collar and grabbed a cord from the table of wares. She stepped closer to Cracker, saw Mike at the door watching what was happening, and Tabby told Cracker, "Tie them to the ends of this cord, I'm gonna hang 'em around my neck!" She stood, holding the coat wide open as Cracker hung the shotguns, muzzle down, the cord behind her neck and the shotguns hanging over her chest. Tabby nodded, pulled the coat closed, buttoned one button and walked out the door.

As she suspected, Cord was coming from his office, ready to make the rounds of the town as he usually did this time of day, but he had no sooner stepped into the street to cross over, than a shout came, "Sheriff! You kilt muh brother an' I'm gonna kill you!"

Cord stopped, frowned as he looked up the street to see two men, one in a derby the other with a flat brimmed felt hat. Both had rifles cradled in their arms, but the derby moved closer to the side, stepped up on the boardwalk, and stood watching. Cord's attention turned to the talker, "Who are you and who was your brother?" he called out.

"I'm Sam Wright an' muh brother was Newt Morrison!"

"Were you ridin' with Morrison when he was a Red Leg?"

"That's right. But I wasn't there when you kilt

him. But I was there when you an' Moses had your fight." As he talked, he slowly walked closer, yet kept his rifle held across his chest. He was a good forty yards away, but still coming. Cord stopped in the middle of the street, his arms across his chest, his duster open and his hand resting on the butt of his pistol that sat in the holster on his left hip. He shook his head slowly, let a sigh escape, until the door of the mercantile slammed open, and Tabby came out.

Tabby looked up the street at the man in the street and the other one on the boardwalk. A quick glance showed the man in the alleyway to Cord's left, but she could not see the one on the same side of the street where she stood. She put her hand to her mouth, cried out, "No, no, no!" and started running to Cord. Crying out as loud as she could, "No, no, no! You can't kill my husband! He's all I've got! No, please, no!" she pleaded as she ran to Cord.

Cord frowned, looked from Tabby to Wright and back to Tabby, "No! No Tabby! Stay back!" he called, holding out one hand as if to stop her.

She ran into his arms, hugged him tight and spoke just loud enough for him to hear. "There's a shotgun hanging in my coat! Take one—it's loaded! There's two others, in the alleys on both sides!" and held onto him with one arm visibly around his neck, the other grabbing the second shotgun. Cord slipped the knot on the cord, grabbed the shotgun, lowered it to his side, then said loudly, "Woman! Get to the side!" and appeared to shove her away.

Tabby stumbled purposely, her back to the outlaws, the frock coat and full dress obscuring their view of her shotgun. Cord had also turned to the side, keeping the shotgun down along his leg, and lifted one hand toward Sam Wright and Willy Vanhorn, "You don't need to do this! You're gonna die just like your brother if you keep coming!" warned Cord.

But Wright was determined and had to make his move. He was counting on Finnegan and Plummer, who had taken positions in the alleyways between buildings, and Vanhorn, who sided him from the boardwalk to his right. But he was alone in the middle of the roadway that divided the town. The man standing before him was supposed to cower and beg, but he stood, not even straightaway facing him, his side to him and he was pointing at him, threatening him.

Wright growled, started to lift his rifle and shouted, "Kill him!"

But the only blast and roar came from the sheriff as he lifted the double-barreled Greener shotgun and cut loose with both barrels. The shotgun bucked, roared, blasted and spat death with a heavy load of double-aught buckshot. The first barrel was for Sam Wright. The blast whistled through the air and slammed into the middle of Wright, ripping his rifle from his hands and tearing its way through his coat, his belt, and blossomed blood across his front. He seemed to lay back as his feet lifted off the ground and his coat tail flared, but when he hit the dirt, dust was the only thing moving.

Without any hesitation, Cord dropped to one knee as he turned slightly to the right and triggered the second barrel just as the cowboy called Parker Finnegan stepped into the open with rifle raised but was met with a load of about eight or nine .33 caliber double-aught buckshot that ripped through his pretty face, neck and chest, knocking him to his back in the dirt.

Tabby whirled to her left, went down on one knee, although it was not as easy as she was used to, but even with feet tangled in the hem of her long skirt, she brought up the Greener and let the first blast spread its wings and buckshot as it sought the target of Vanhorn. Standing beside a porch post, he was still open to the charge of double-aught shot and eight out of nine of the .33 caliber lead balls found purchase as they tore into the torso of the would-be gambler, and he lost his last hand of poker. He grabbed at the post, but blood covered his hands. He looked down at his middle to see nothing but blood. He tried to look down the street but saw only a woman who appeared to have fallen in the street. He frowned, confused, "a woman?" and fell on his face to slide to the ground from the boardwalk.

Tabby knew the other one of the four was in the alleyway between her and her last target, and she quickly twisted toward that opening, but the blast from a big Sharps Buffalo gun came from the doorway of the mercantile, and Cracker's grin was almost as big as the door as he watched his target get lifted off his feet, bent in the middle and land on his rear, blood spurting from his chest and he slumped forward. "Got him!" declared a triumphant Cracker, grinning at Cord and Tabby.

Cord rose and moved the three steps to his woman, lifted her to her feet, and said, "Thanks, Deputy!" He grinned as he pulled her close and gave her a thankful embrace.

She spoke in his ear, "You ruined my new dress!"

Cord stepped back, looked at his disheveled woman, "Nah, you're prettier'n ever an' I love you just like you are!"

She looked down at the dress, the hem torn and dragging, dirt across the skirt, looked at Cord, "Oh well, the coat's nice," she said, and laughed.

33

PREPARATIONS

THE BARLOW AND SANDERSON STAGE ROCKED AND rattled into Oro City, dragging a billowing cloud of dust behind it. As it pulled up at the stage station, which was an extension of the livery stable, they were greeted by the Stage agent, standing at the hitchrail and trying to fan the dust from his face. There were only two passengers that climbed from the stage, both men and the opposite of one another. The first man out appeared to be a man of confidence and purpose. He had on a wool suit with vest and pin-stripe trousers, a derby, and a heavy frock coat draped over his arm. He stopped, looked around, and upon seeing the stage agent, he nodded and pushed his way past to enter the station office. The second man looked to be a merchant or peddler of some sort and when he spotted the mercantile, he started at a quick step to cross the roadway and go to the business.

Cord was watching from his chair that sat on the boardwalk in front of his office, and he continued his observations with a touch of disinterest, thinking more about going home for his lunch with Tabby. There were a few seasonal sourdoughs that were gathering at the station, warbags in hand and buying tickets. This would probably be the last stage out of Oro City for the season. With winter coming on, the stage line usually suspended regular runs until green up, with only a rare run, weather permitting. Miners that could not work their placer claims in the winter, preferred to go to the lower and warmer climes or even return from whence they came to reunite with families.

As the hostler was busy changing out the six-up team, the driver and messenger went to the café, and the station keeper started toward the sheriff's office, a frown on his face and a hurry-up to his pace. He stopped before the sheriff, hands on hips, and declared, "Sheriff, we need a guard for the stage. The messenger ain't 'nuff. There's a considerable gold shipment goin' out and some o' the miners are packin' their year's take, and it's an all-fired risk! We gotta have help! So, I was thinkin', if you'd agree to go, the stage comp'ny would pay you a bonus an' you'd only be goin' no further'n Cañon City."

"How far's Cañon City?" asked Cord, remembering going through there, but that was some time ago.

"It's 'bout a hunnert'n twenty miles, two, three

days at most. One way, that is." He paused, looking around and back at Cord, "You see, sheriff, there's more'n a hunnert thousand dollars' worth o' gold goin' out, and the driver said they seen some suspicious lookin' characters down to Granite and such, so..." he shrugged. His nervousness added to his urgency and plea.

"What time ya' leavin'?"

The clerk pulled out his pocket watch, looked at Cord, "In 'bout an hour."

"I'll go talk to my wife, have me somethin' to eat, and I'll be back. Now, I ain't sayin' I'm goin', but I'll consider it."

"Oh, thank you, Sheriff, thank you!" declared the clerk and spun on his heel and started back to the station.

"But you'll be gone for most of a week!" declared Tabby as she poured Cord's coffee cup full of the steaming brew. "But..." she paused, stepped back and looked at Cord with a mischievous smile, "Maybe I could go along and we could, well, call it a honeymoon trip."

She chuckled as she turned away to fetch Cord's plate and food. As she turned back to face him, he was leaning back in his chair, grinning, "That's not a bad idea. But...well, I don't know. The reason they want a guard is because of some *suspicious-looking characters* the driver saw along the way back toward Granite and beyond."

"Two guards are better'n one! And I could travel *incognito.*"

Cord frowned, "That's a big word for hidin' out."

Tabby laughed, "Eat up, an' I'll go get ready."

"Can't take much, just one haversack for the both of us!" he declared as he bowed his head for a short prayer of thanksgiving, but as he prayed, he added a plea for protection and a safe journey.

————

THE STAGE ROCKED BACK on its traces as the six-up leaned into the collars and harness. The driver cracked his whip as the team straightened out and lifted heads to get the coach moving. The road took them west out of town and at the mouth of California Gulch, the driver pulled on the leads to make the sharp bend in the road and head south. The coach road would follow the river all the way to Cañon City, but Cord had learned they would probably overnight at Cleora before entering the canyon of the Arkansas River for the remainder of the trip.

The trail lay in the bottom of the valley, towering peaks rising high into the clouds on the west, timber-covered hills and buttes on the east, and the stage road followed the river south. About seven miles out of Oro City, the hills began to crowd closer to the river, the timbered skirts of the mountain peaks carrying the remaining gold of the aspen and dropping the leaves into the runoff creeks. It was at Two-bit Gulch that the valley narrowed to no more than a gulch itself. The stage road hugged the flanks of the hills on the east side of the river until they arrived at the first stage stop at Granite. The dust of fifteen miles had settled on Cord's shoulders as he rode atop the stage, sitting behind the driver and messenger with his feet on the bench seat between them. The driver called out, "Granite stop! We're just changing teams, but you might wanna stretch yore legs!"

Cord dropped to the ground, opened the door for Tabby and helped her out. She was wearing her split skirt under the long duster. She had explained, "These are better for travelin' on the stage, and for keeping my pistol and such out of sight." She had been determined to have her new Greener shotgun within reach and kept it between the seat cushion and the edge of the stage door. With a short stop for necessities and the change of the team, the stage was back on the road by mid-afternoon.

Cord leaned forward and asked, "Where's the next stop?"

"It's called Riverside. Ain't much, sits along Cottonwood Creek," explained the driver. He glanced back to Cord over his shoulder, "By the way, most folks call me Tater!" and nodded as he focused his attention on the team.

Cord chuckled, thinking the name fit because he was shaped like a big potato. Cord asked, "I was told you saw some outlaw types on your way north.

Whereabouts?" Both men had to shout to be heard over the rattle of trace chains, the creak and groan of the rocking coach on the braces, and the rumble of the wheels on the rocky road.

"Twas at a place some are callin' Centreville. It's where Chalk Creek comes down from the mountains, good land thereabouts, an' a few folks are tryin' to make of go of it. There was three of 'em, one big colored fella, but he was dressed good for a colored man. Another'n kind of a dandy, if'n you know what I mean. The third, well, weren't nuthin' special 'bout him. But they reined up when we passed, nodded an' waved, but...there was just sumpin' 'bout 'em, kinda made muh skin crawl, if'n you know what I mean. From the looks of things, I th'ot they mighta had a camp down the crick a ways." He lifted the long bull whip, cracked it over the heads of the six-up as if to emphasize what he said as much as to keep the team moving.

"Yeah, I know what'chu mean. Might be I even know them fellas. Run into 'em b'fore and they ain't what'chu call upstandin' citizens." Cord chuckled to himself, remembering his fight with Moses, the big colored man. He never had any encounters with the dandy, Chauncey Tittle, but he knew they had been a part of the bunch of Red Legs.

And the driver was right when he said the River- side stop was not much. It was only a log building, sod roof, lean-to barn and corrals. A scruffy station keeper came from the cabin, scowling and scratching as he walked to the team and began unhitching the six horses. Tater leaned over and called to the passengers, "Riverside! Quick stop, outhouse 'roun' back, make it quick. Ain't got no time to be wastin'!" he declared as he wrapped the reins around the brake lever and climbed down. Cord followed, leaving his Greener up top, and going to the door to give Tabby a hand down.

For a slow-moving scruffy-looking sort, the station keeper made good time harnessing the new team and before everyone was done with their little walk around the station, the driver had mounted up and hollered, "Get a move on! We're burnin' daylight!" Cord had already seen Tabby to her seat inside and climbed up top himself. He chuckled at the shout of the driver, leaned forward to ask the messenger, "He always that cantankerous?"

"Him?" he asked, "He's in a good mood today!" laughed the messenger. He looked back at Cord, extended his hand to shake, "I'm Bones, got that handle when I was but a pup, I was really skinny then." He laughed, shaking his head as Cord accepted his hand and replied with, "I'm Cord. Is that all you hafta do, is blow that bugle whenever we get near a station?"

"Purty much. That an' keep the driver awake," he chuckled, knowing there was little chance of a driver getting to snooze as he handled the lines of the team. "Some messengers carry a shotgun, kinda look the part of a guard, but I don't. I just blow this!" he lifted the bugle that hung below his right arm on a long cord. "Whenever there are special dispatches, like from the bosses, law officers, the army an' such, I'm supposed to hold 'em up here, keep track of 'em, hand 'em off personal like."

The driver added, as he reached for the lines, "Yeah, he ain't good for much, but he keeps me comp'ny when we ain't got many passengers. Other'n that, he's a mite worthless," grinned the driver, looking from Bones to Cord and back as he grabbed the bullwhip and reared back to crack it over the team to get started back on the road. Tater sat on the right, clearing the way for his whip, and with Bones on the left, Cord sat with his feet on the seat between them while he rode up top.

34

CONFRONTATION

THE STAGE ROAD HAD HUGGED THE WEST BANK OF THE river as they came from Granite moving south. After the Centreville stop, the stage road bent a little to the west, well in the shadow of the towering granite peaks of the Sawatch Range, and took to the flats away from the dark canyon of the river as it roared through what Tater called Brown's Canyon. "Yeah, it's cuz o' the crick that comes from the mountains yonder," nodding to the sky scratchers off his right shoulder, "is called Brown Creek. There's some settlers trying to put in farms and ranches and such out in these flats. Mebbe they'll make it, mebbe not," pronounced the prairie philosopher, with a chuckle at his homespun wisdom.

The road was easy traveling, the land flat and the pull easy for the fresh team. But after about three miles, they crossed a little no-name creek no more than three feet wide and only a few inches deep, and climbed the north slope of a wide plateau that fell from high mountains. The road stretched across the flat of the grassy plateau that was dotted with the growths of cottonwood trees that were doing their best to match colors with mountain aspen, fluttering their gold hued leaves in the slight breeze that whispered across the flat.

Another mile and the road dropped over the shoulder of the plateau into a green gulch that looked to be less than a half-mile wide. A line of trees cut the gulch in half as it followed the little creek on its way to join its big brother, the Arkansas River. But it was as the stage neared this long line of cottonwoods that three masked horsemen moved across the road to block the way. They sat their mounts with rifles pointed at the stage and as Tater reined up, the big man of the bunch growled, "You done the right thing, driver. Now, my partner's gonna come alongside while your messenger there gets that strongbox outta the boot there and drops it to the ground." Cord watched as the second man, attired in a dark frock coat over a brocade vest and wearing a flat-brimmed black hat and a colorful bandanna over his mouth, nudged his mount forward toward the left side of the stage. The third man moved toward the other side. Cord rapped his knuckles on the right side, giving Tabby the heads up for that side and he slowly slid his Greener across his legs, muzzle to his left side.

When the man neared, he called up, "You heard

him! Get that strongbox down here!" The messenger squirmed around, "Uh, there ain't one!" he whined, holding his hands out, palms up, to his side.

Cord spoke just loud enough for the masked man to hear, "Uh, you need to drop your rifle and lift your hands, or I'll blast you off your horse with this double-barreled Greener loaded with double-aught buckshot!"

The surprised outlaw glared, looked down to see the two-eyed monster of a man-killer staring at him with black eyes, then looked up at Cord, who was grinning and nodding slightly. Cord had seen the third man moving toward the right side of the stage, his rifle butt on his thigh, and heard the clatter of hooves on rocks and knew he was within range of Tabby and her shotgun. He heard her speak, but too soft for him to understand her words, but he knew she had done the same with the third man.

Cord looked down at the dandy and said, "Well?"

The outlaw glared and started to lift his rifle, but Cord pulled the triggers on the big Greener, and the roar of the shotgun was matched by the roar from Tabby's shotgun and both men were knocked from their saddles, their stomachs and chests peppered with eighteen .33 caliber lead balls that destroyed any semblance of clothing and drove the two men from their saddles as if they had been struck by a charging buffalo. Their horses spooked, jerked back, lowered their heads between their front feet and started bucking as they tried to kick a hole in heaven in the doing of it.

The third man was startled by the blasts from the shotguns, and his horse spooked sideways, almost unseating the big man, but when his horse joined in the bucking contest, he dropped his rifle and did his best to keep his seat. The big horse took his own way and crashed through the cottonwoods and willows beside the creek, and the last time he was seen was just ahead of a rolling dust cloud a long way downstream. Cord looked around, watching the empty saddles waving their stirrups at the clouds and the two riderless horses lose their get-up and go and settle down, standing spraddle legged and looking at one another, sides heaving, heads hanging, and nostrils flared as they sucked wind. The two outlaws that had taken the shotgun blasts, lay where they fell, unmoving, staring with sightless eyes at the slow-moving clouds overhead.

The driver had kept a tight rein of the six-up, talking to them to settle them down as the messenger jumped down and went to the leaders to hold their bridles and stroke their faces to keep them still. Tater looked over his shoulder at Cord, "Was that just you that did all that shootin'?"

"Nah. My wife was inside and she got that'n," nodding to the remains of the skinny outlaw.

"Your wife? I din't even know she was armed!" declared Tater, shaking his head. "What'chu wanna do with them?" motioning to the bodies with his elbow.

"Leave 'em be. We don't have time for a buryin', 'sides, we don't know if that other'n'll be comin' back. Get Bones back aboard and let's get on with it."

"Yo! Bones! Come on! We're gonna skedaddle outta here!" shouted Tater.

Cord jumped down and caught up the two horses, tied them to the back of the stage, climbed back aboard and nodded to Tater. "Take it easy for a while, give them horses a chance to catch their breath."

———

THE REST of the way was easygoing. After topping out on the plateau above the creek and the site of the attempted robbery, the terrain was a little hilly with low rises and draws covered with lots of juniper and piñon. The stage road bent a little to the east and moved closer to the river, crossed over the rickety bridge and stayed on the flats that skirted the hills on the east of the valley. As the shoulders of the hills nudged closer to the river, the stage road hugged the narrow shoulder that stood above the river and soon rounded a point to show the stage stop and more of Cleora.

Tater turned a little to talk over his shoulder to Cord, "We'll be over-nightin' at Cleora. Are you gonna go on with us to Cañon City?"

"I think we just took care of your problem, didn't we?"

Tater chuckled, "Yeah, I reckon."

"Then we'll be taking those horses," nodding to the ones from the outlaws—"and gettin' on back home to Oro City, but not till mornin'." Cord grinned as Tater wrapped the reins of the team around the brake handle.

"Howdy folks! Step on down, come inside. The wife's got a good meal waitin' and we've got liquid libations to suit everyone!" declared a man who looked to be pushing forty, a slight paunch under a broad chest and shoulders. He had a wide grin, clean-shaven face, and a full head of brown hair that was parted down the middle. He wore a leather vest over a homespun shirt and denim britches. He had a jovial smile and eyes that danced with mischief. He stepped back to let the few passengers into the building that had a sign over the door reading *Bale House*. And another sign to the side announced this was the *South Arkansas Stage Stop*.

Cord dropped to the ground, helped Tabby from the stage, and as they stood together, he looked at William Bale, who still stood with his thumbs in his pockets as he watched the folks leave the stage and go to the rambling log house that was their home and the stage station. Cord asked, "What's the name of this place?"

"Cleora, named it after muh youngest daughter!"

chuckled William. "C'mon in folks, make yourself to home!"

"What do we do to get a room for the night?"

"Same as the rest, just let muh wife know, she'll assign you a room upstairs. Only cost you a dollar!" he declared, grinning broadly.

Cord looked at Tabby, "You go on in. I'll put up these horses. We'll be takin' 'em back to Oro City in the mornin' and I want 'em to have some grain."

Tabby smiled, nodded, and started for the door. Cord turned away, went to the stage and untied the two horses, led them to the barn, and finding a couple empty stalls, began stripping off the gear. After a good rub down and a roll in the dust, the horses stood, shook and eagerly went into the stalls where Cord had put some grain in the feed bins. After stacking the gear in the corner, Cord gave everything a last once-over, and satisfied, headed for the house.

35

RETURN

WITH AN EARLY START, CORD AND TABBY MADE GOOD TIME riding back north toward Oro City, but they knew this would be at least a two-day ride, but they were glad to be aboard horses instead of the rattling, rocking stage. Tabby said, "I still feel dusty after riding in that stage!" she declared, smacking her duster and raising a little bit of a dust cloud.

"I think I might have an answer for that," grinned Cord, for he, too, had eaten enough dust to last a lifetime.

Tabby saw the grin on Cord's face, knew he was up to something, and she smiled, "Alright, let's have it. What do you have cooking in that devious mind of yours?"

"You'll see, you'll see," he chuckled. They had taken a short break at high noon, sought out some shade and munched on some jerky, but it was little enough. Both wanted to make good time and make this a two-day trip home rather than a drawn-out three days.

When they passed the site of the attempted hold-up, buzzards were circling, and both buzzards and other carrion eaters were having their fill on the bodies of the outlaws, but Cord swung wide of the sight and pointed to the flats beyond the creek where a narrow trail, seldom used, took to the flats above the river that sided the stage road. It was easy going, and they kicked up several jackrabbits, saw a couple coyotes conspiring together about their next rabbit feast, jumped a couple mule deer out of the brush along a narrow creek, and the trail kept slanting to the west, drawing closer to the timbered skirts of the towering mountains.

Tabby frowned as she looked at the treetops of the spruce, pine, and juniper trees that edged the black timber that climbed the towering mountains. There appeared to be a thin smoke, no, steam rising beyond the trees, apparently coming from the long draw that split the mountains. She frowned, looked at Cord, "What are you up to?"

Cord chuckled, "I was talkin' to the stage driver when we came through this valley before. He pointed out this place, said there were mineral hot springs that the natives liked to bathe in, said it was mighty refreshing!" He grinned at her, saw her expression change to one of joy and anticipation as she dug heels into her mount's ribs and kicked him to a trot to get to the hot springs.

Steam rose from the springs, lifting the thin cloud of vapors high above the valley floor. A narrow stream came from the pool below the steam cloud and carried its own veil of steam as it trickled down the slight slope and into the stream that came from the deep canyon that split the mountains. Tabby nudged her mount closer, grinned at Cord and jumped to the ground. She led the horse to the edge of the trees, tied him off within reach of some graze and trotted to the pool, kicking off her boots, and shedding the duster. As she neared the edge of the water, she cautiously stuck her toes into the shallow ripples at the edge of the deeper pond, lowered her foot deeper into it, turned and smiled at Cord, as she started shedding the rest of her clothes.

Cord stood at the edge of the water, smiling as Tabby ducked under, then turned around to look up and down the valley, watchful of any danger. He knew this was a hot springs pool that was often used by the natives, and this was also an area for grizzly bear, black bear, mountain lions, and many predators of the two-legged variety. It would not do for both of them to be defenseless in the water and have something threaten their safety. He had learned long ago to always err on the side of safety and good judgment.

Tabby sat on a rock, smiling and happy, clean

clothes on, comfortable, as she watched Cord take his dip in the hot springs pool. The rifle leaned against her leg, and she looked around at the high-rising mountains, the shoulder of rugged cliffs on the far side of the valley and the distant green of the valley below. She knew those colors were rapidly changing, with the nearby aspen already shedding their golden coats of fluttering leaves. It was a beautiful time in the Rocky Mountains, and she reveled in the beauty, their new life together, and the prospects of a stable future. She was happy, pulled her knees up, hugged them and then Cord came from the steamy waters, and she chuckled.

They spent the night near the mouth of the valley that split the mountains with the Cottonwood Creek, rose early and were on the trail north as the sun struggled to rise above the timber covered hills on the east side of the valley. They rode side by side, sharing every moment and quiet thought as they dreamed of their future together—a family, a home and more.

They passed through Granite with nothing more than a wave and a nod. As the day waned, the valley of the Arkansas River began to widen and open up, and the sun was nearing the tips of the mountain peaks in the west. The massive alluvial fan lay below the mountains, spreading into the valley with rich soil that showed grassy flats and it was from the edge of that flatland that a line of mule deer were cautiously making their way to the river for their evening drink. Cord reined up, and Tabby leaned back to slip the Winchester from the scabbard. She slid to the ground and dropped to one knee, using her other knee for a leaning rest and sighted in on a young buck that was off to the side of the others, dropping his head, looking for graze.

Tabby sighted in, Cord watching, and as she pulled the trigger, the buck lifted his head, but the bullet flew true and drove into its heart, entering just behind the front leg. The buck took a step, staggered, and went down. The rest of the deer scattered and disappeared into the trees. Cord grinned, Tabby stood and smiled at her man and said, "Now, it's your turn!"

"My turn?"

"Ummhmm, we need to get him dressed out, loaded, and get back home while we still have some light," she said, nodding to the slow-setting sun that was already beginning to paint the western sky with colors. "So, we better hurry!" she smiled, giggled and slipped the rifle back in the scabbard and swung aboard her mount.

———

THEY RODE up the street of Oro City to the greetings and cheers of the residents. Many calling out, "Welcome back, Sheriff!" and waving as they rode toward the edge of town. When they stopped in front of their house, Cord tied off the horses, slipped the carcass of the deer from behind his saddle, and with it over his shoulder, carried it to the back porch and dropped it outside the door to the kitchen. Tabby had stepped down, taken the parfleche from behind her saddle, and with rifle and shotgun under one arm, the parfleche in the other hand, she made it to the front porch where she dropped everything. Cord came from behind the house, saw her on the porch, "I'll take the horses to the livery and be right back."

"You want me to fix some supper?"

"Of course, I'm hungry, aren't you?"

She smiled, nodded, and watched as Cord stepped aboard his horse, grabbed the reins of hers and started to the livery. By the time he returned, she already had the stove fired up, coffee on, and had cut the backstrap from the deer and sliced it into steaks that she was preparing for supper. Cord walked into the kitchen, sat down with Blue at his side, and reached down to stroke the dog behind his ears. He looked up at Tabby, "I think he missed us!"

"I missed having him along."

"Yeah, me too. But...looks like we'll have time to settle in before winter does, so I'm lookin' forward to some lazy days in the winter. How 'bout you?"

She smiled, nodded, "Ummhmm. It will be good to have more time for ourselves, you know, just us, together, not worryin' about all the rest of things."

"Yeah, but I still have a job to do," he added, touching the sheriff's badge on his chest.

"Ahh, that's nothin'. We can handle that!"

"Oh, *we* can, can *we?*" he grinned, pouring himself a cup of coffee.

She came near, slipped her arms around his middle, pushed against him, looked up at him and said, "Yes, *we* can!"

A LOOK AT:
THE COVENANT

From the bestselling author of The Plainsman Western series comes a 2024 Independent Press Award Distinguished Favorite for Historical Fiction—an exciting and explosive new Western series.

It is a time of uncertainty in the infancy of a growing nation. The Wild West is open and beckoning to displaced men and families, many of whom choose to travel to the unsettled frontier, dreaming of new homes, land, and even riches. But few reckon on those who have lived in those lands for centuries—the native peoples. Blackfoot, Crow, Sioux, and more.

Elijah McCain, fresh from the Union army where he attained the rank of Lieutenant Colonel with the Mounted Rifles—a cavalry unit under General Sherman—has returned home to find his wife on her deathbed, pleading for her twin sons. She elicits a promise, a covenant, from her husband: "Find our boys, and bring them home."

So, Eli vows to do just that. Holding her hand as she slips from life, he promises to bring their sons home—no matter what. Even if it's the undoing of dreams, lives, and more.

AVAILABLE NOW

ABOUT THE AUTHOR

Born and raised in Colorado into a family of ranchers and cowboys, B.N. Rundell is the youngest of seven sons. Juggling bull riding, skiing, and high school, graduation was a launching pad for a hitch in the Army Paratroopers. After the army, he finished his college education in Springfield, MO, and together with his wife and growing family, entered the ministry as a Baptist preacher.

With many years as a successful pastor and educator, he retired from the ministry and followed in the footsteps of his entrepreneurial father and started a successful insurance agency, which is now in the hands of his trusted nephew. Having finally realized his life-long dream, B.N. has turned his efforts to writing a variety of books, from children's picture books and young adult adventure books, to the historical fiction and Western genres, which are his first loves.